BRAHMINISM
WEAPONS TO FIGHT
COUNTER REVOLUTION

BRAHMINISM
WEAPONS TO FIGHT
COUNTER REVOLUTION

V.T. Rajshekar

ISBN : 978-81-212-1296-0

First Published, 2015

Published by

Gyan Publishing House
5, Ansari Road, Darya Ganj,
New Delhi- 110 002
Ph. : 011-47340999, 9811692060
E-mail: books@gyanbooks.com

Cataloging in Publication Data—DK
   Courtesy: D.K. Agencies (P) Ltd. <docinfo@dkagencies.com>

Rajshekar Shetty, V. T., 1932- author.
   Brahminism : weapons to fight counter revolution / V.T. Rajshekar.
     pages cm
     Reprint.
     ISBN 9788121212960

   1. Brahmanism—Controversial literature.   I. Title.

DDC 294.5   23

Edited and enlarged version of the valedictory speech
delivered at the 3-day seminar on "Brahminism",
March 14-16, 2003, at the Indian Social Institute,
Bangalore, India.

Contents

CHAPTER-I

Introduction

I sat through the entire three days of a "Seminar on Brahminism" in Bangalore (India) from March 14 to 16, 2003 and I can tell you that the different experts who spoke on the subject gave a very gripping, very touching descriptions of the horrors of Brahminism. I admire their ability to identify the Enemy and also their description of the ways this Enemy is persecuting us and how this Enemy is silently killing us with its poison of Brahminism. The speakers gave a very heart-rending description of the pain and sufferings the victims of Brahminism are undergoing.

To put it in medical language, I can say the different experts (call them specialist doctors) have given us the different symptoms of the disease. I listened to their very elaborate descriptions of the symptoms, their narrations of the intensity of the pain, and all the different features of this deadly disease called Brahminism. Yes. What I heard during the three days was a very accurate, very touching description of the different symptoms of the disease.

Islam & Christianity

The experts have said the patient is suffering from a particular disease (Brahminism). And because of this disease, he is not getting sleep, he has no appetite, he has unbearable pain all over the body, high temperature — all sorts of suffering.

Brahminism has been troubling us from birth to death and even after death. Brahminism is about 3,000 years old and during this period it took several names, put on different dresses. The latest name is RSS (Rashtriya Swayamsevak Sangh). Brahminism is not an ideology. It is an anti-human thought, a mental disease. Budhism rejected Brahminism but was later swallowed by it. Every social movement in India, right from the days of Charvaka and Jainism, was against Brahminism. But Brahminism defeated every protest movement and Budhism, Jainism. Sikhism, Veerashaivism — all got Brahminised. Even Christianity and Islam are getting Brahminised. No religion has escaped the influence of Brahminism. If India is poor and suffering, it is because of Brahminism. All of us have failed to fight Brahminism. This is what the seminar participants said.

Many foreign invaders poured into India. All of them merged with the local indigenous population. The only people who refused to merge but maintained their distinct identity, their aloofness were the Aryan Brahmins. Even the Aryan Kshatriyas and Vaishyas got themselves diluted but not the Brahmins. This is what they said.

Hinduism becomes a minority religion

Brahminism stands for falsehood, treachery, deception. These are the weapons they use to keep the indigenous people as slaves. Divide and rule was not a British invention but that of Brahmins. The custom of burning the dead is a Brahmin custom. Since the Brahmins had no homeland of their own, they had no land to bury their dead. Hence they resorted to burning their dead, they said.

Brahminism claims Hinduism (the latest name for their religion, if it can be called a religion, though the Supreme Court of India called it a way of life) as the only non-violent religion of the world. If this is correct why all the Hindu gods in our temple architecture and painting carry deadly weapons?

The Charvakas were the first people to condemn the entire Brahminical scriptures as false. Brahmins used the *Puranas* to fool the non-Brahmins. The Vedas and all other scriptures were full of contradictions. Islam today reigned in 48 countries of the world. Christianity is all over the world. But Hinduism, claiming to be the oldest religion of the world, is confined only to India though it is older than both Christianity and Islam. Even inside India it is getting weaker. The Hindus themselves fear that by the end of the 21st century, their "majority religion" of Hinduism will be reduced to a minority. Even the name of this so-called religion, Hinduism, was given by the Muslims. This Hindu *Dharma* has no founder, no single sacred text. It has not even a name. It has no single god. And yet they call it a religion. They say beef-eating is prohibited under Hinduism but when their god Rama with brother Lakshmana came to sage Vasista's home, he cut the youngest calf and cooked it to feed the god who immensely enjoyed it. This is said in their own *Ramayana*. Beef-eating was then the exclusive privilege of the Brahmins. Vatsayana recommended beef-eating. It was the Adi Shankara who stopped beef-eating to kill Budhism, they said. (*Dalit Voice* June 1, 2003 p. 14: "*Beef-eating during vedic period*"). This is what they said in the seminar.

Reject *vaidik* gods

Brahmins say "merit" is their exclusive monopoly. Then why Kalidasa, Vyasa, Valmiki were all Dalits? Why no Brahmin could create any great scripture? Why Brahmins could not produce a Dr. Babasaheb Ambedkar, they asked.

Brahminism today is our Enemy No.1. Brahmins are ruling us today because they are an alert community. They used literacy and education as their weapons to beat us — and by keeping us out of it.

We have to reject all the *vaidik* gods and go back to our native, *desi* deities. All *vaidik* gods are exploiters, they said. One speaker said:

> There is nothing like Brahminism without the Brahmin. "Brahminism cannot be separated from the Brahmin. Brahminism came from the Brahmin only. If you are a Hindu, you cannot escape from Brahminism. Though the *Gayatri Mantra* was made by Viswamitra, the Brahmins never gave him the honour because he was not a Brahmin. The *Gayatri Mantra* has now become the property of the Brahmins. The correct name of Hinduism is *Vaidik Dharma*. We non-Brahmins have taken to Hinduism without being Hindu. We have all become the concubines of a man calling himself Brahmin. Right from the days of the Vedas, the Brahmin has done one thing: that is preserving his supreme position".

Brahmins possess lots and lots of information but they did not produce a single intellectual. They had no social concern. Swami Vivekananda, who made Hinduism famous all over the world, had bitterly criticised Brahmins. Today it is the non-Brahmins who are carrying the Brahmin on their heads. During the *Dipavali* festival, we burn Bali Chakravarti who saved us and India from Brahminism. Brahmins killed Bali by using the dwarf Brahmin Vamana, they said.

Dayananda Saraswati killed

Brahmins never support social change because social change will wipe out the poverty of India. Dayananda Saraswati, a Gujarati Brahmin, was killed by the Brahmins for trying to reform Hinduism through his Arya Samaj. Brahmins also hated Vivekananda because he was a *shudra*, they said. Brahminism is more powerful and more dangerous than the atom bomb. It has caused more violence and bloodshed than all the world wars put together.

This is the essence of the criticisms made by the different speakers at the seminar. (DV April 16, 2003 p.7: "*Brahminism can't be cured & hence endured?*").

The speakers were C.S. Dwarakanath, Advocate, Fr. Albert and

Chand Peer of the Indian Social Institute, Prof. K.S. Bhagavan, Mysore University, Nidumamidi Swami, Prof. Shivrudra Kallolikar, C.S. Laxmi, M.C. Raj, Prof. Ambrose Pinto of St. Joseph's College, Bangalore, Dr. Samata Deshmane of Bangalore University, Sridhar, editor of the *Agni*, Prof. Narasimhaiya, Agrahara Krishnamurthy, Prof. Lohitaswa, Kalle Sivothama Rao, Prof. Hasan Mansoor, President of the Karnataka PUCL, Ju.Ho. Narayanaswamy, Prof. Mogalli Ganesh, P.S. Sridhara Murthy, Mrs. Jyoti Raj, Mrs. Vijaya Mahesh, Mrs. Amrita Athradi, Prof. Babu Mathew of National Law University, Bangalore, Prof, Ravi Verma Kumar, Advocate, Bangalore, Dr. Banjagere Jayaprakash and many other scholars.

All the speeches were good and full of criticisms of the Brahmins and their Brahminism. But not a single speaker provided the remedies to cure the disease of Brahminism.

Anti-woman practices

The speakers, however, did not go into the anti-woman practices under Brahminism. Even a Brahmin woman is a *shudra*. She has no right to wear the "sacred thread" and hence cannot become a temple priest. Even the wife of a temple priest cannot enter the *sanctum sanctorum* (*garbha gudi*) of a temple. Brahminism sanctions all sorts of punishments against the woman including the Brahmin woman. She has no right to inherit the parental property. Dr. Babasaheb Ambedkar as India's first Law Minister introduced the Hindu Code Bill to confer equal rights on Hindu women but the Bill was opposed by all Brahmin men including the Brahmin Prime Minister Nehru but supported by all Brahmin women MPs in India's Parliament. Facing powerful brahminical opposition, Dr. Ambedkar resigned as Minister on this issue. Such is the power of the male under Brahminism — fully sanctioned by the *Manudharma Sastra*.

Brahminism sanctions *sati* (widow-burning), dowry, child marriage, prostitution, *Devadasi* (a system of temple prostitution of Untouchable girls). The declining sex ratio in India due to mass female foeticide is a widespread practice in all parts of India. Death of females is already weakening India's social fabric. Brahminism prefers boys. This is the practice among the upper castes (Hindus) who are the most educated people of India. The list of anti-women practices under Brahminism is too long.

These specialist doctors (at the seminar) have spoken only of the symptoms. But what is the use of diagnosing the symptoms without diagnosing the disease? Hence as an expert on this disease, I do not want to talk of the symptoms but diagnose the disease, prescribe you the right medicines so that we get a permanent cure for this disease.

Saving the Brahmin from Brahminism

Hence I speak on the "Horrors of Brahminism" and provide a guidebook to fight and destroy Brahminism and to those wanting to save Brahmins and also India from this deadliest disease known in human history.

So my speech will be entirely different from the rest of the speakers.

After having worked in the *Indian Express* for 25 years and later as the Editor of *Dalit Voice* for another 23 years, I am of the opinion that there can be no Brahminism without the Brahmin. He changes his dress very often, assumes different names, propounds different theories and philosophies, talks different languages at different points of time to hide himself and confuse the victims of Brahminism.

The Brahmins are only about 3% of the Indian population

(1,000 and odd millions). That means they are a micro-minority. If you just shout loudly, they will catch the first plane and run away to America, their latest fatherland.

Lately, the Brahmin has given a new name to his religion, calling it Hindu and Hinduism. If you go through the Brahminical "Sacred Scriptures", these two words, the Hindu and Hinduism, are no where found. The Supreme Court of India has said Hinduism is not a religion but a way of life.

Brahminism is not only the main problem for the entire country, it is equally a big problem for its very creators, the Brahmins. So, the Brahmins themselves have to be saved from Brahminism. There never will be peace in this subcontinent until the Brahmin himself gets convinced that he is suffering from a disease called Brahminism and that his disease is affecting the health and happiness of all the people of the country.

And his latest catch phrase is "cultural nationalism" — a very dangerous phrase. Only a "nation" can talk about "nationalism". But India itself is not a nation. Every time the indigenous people tried to forge India into a "nation", the Brahminical people came in the way and the nation-formation process was stalled. The natives of India are, therefore, not responsible for shattering the formation of Indian "nation". Dr. Babasaheb Ambedkar has said this with great sorrow.

When India itself is not a nation, how can there be "cultural nationalism"? Whose culture? Whose "nation"? ■

✳ ✳ ✳

CHAPTER - II

Wanted our own media

Go to any Indian village we find no trace of Brahminism there. But what is the picture that we get in a city? The picture of Brahminism. By controlling the cities through their Brahminical monopoly media and the city-based power structures, they give an impression that India is Hindu and its "cultural nationalism" is Hindu. But India is a country of villages.

Do you know who is behind all this game of confusion ? Who is indulging in this mind-manipulation game? It is India's Brahminical media, controlled by its most wicked *vaidik* brains. This media is the total monopoly of Brahminical (upper castes) people.

Role of Media

I have worked in one such media for 25 years and these *vaidiks* conspired and got me dismissed. Today, the entire Brahminical mischief in India is played by this media. This corrupt and idiotic media (with minor exceptions) is the sole cause of all the pain, suffering, deprivation, violence caused by Brahminism. At the same time this media is hiding the perpetrators of this crime but putting the blame on Muslims, Christians etc. This media has created an impression in the "public mind", meaning the newspaper-reading people who constitute not even 30% of India's population, that India's "cultural nationalism" or *Hindutva* is under attack from Muslims and Christians. The state itself is made to tackle the "mischief-mongers" and remove any "threat" to their "cultural nationalism", meaning Brahminism.

Brahminism has established a total control on our thoughts. Not a single announcement can reach the public without the

Brahminical control. The Jews have already shown the power of the media. They control the entire world media. Inside India, the Brahminical forces have shown their power. You control the mind, you control everything including the purse. The instrument of thought will become an educative means. It will tranquilize the public mind to persuade or confuse. If you want to win over your opponents, you must have your own media. Or else you will be defeated. "Public opinion" in India means Brahminical opinion.

But I am sorry to say that not one expert who spoke at the seminar pointed out the mischief of this media. Look at the poverty of the thinking among us. How can we fight the disease when we have not even diagnosed the disease?

Culture jamming

No battle against Brahminism is possible as long as we do not have our own media. All the great revolutionaries who fought against Brahminism, like Dr. Ambedkar, Periyar E.V. Ramaswamy, Dr. R.M. Lohia had their own media. Without your own media, you cannot fight Brahminism which owns India's most powerful media including the electronic media. Those fighting Brahminism may have Justice on their side, Truth on their side. And also majority on their side. But how will they reach Justice and Truth to the people and make it known to them unless you have some media?

In this connection, I congratulate *Agni* Editor Sridhar. He has started a powerful Kannada weekly to fight the Brahminical forces. Victims of Brahminism all over Karnataka must support the *Agni*.

I have talked to leaders of Muslims, Christians, Sikhs. Not once but several times. All of them agreed they were the worst victims of Brahminism. They all said they were suffering because of the poison spread by this Brahminical media. On this point they were all unanimous. But when I told them that we must have a media of our own, they all appreciated my idea, praised me but took no action. This has been going on for the past 10 years, ever since the demolition of the Babri Masjid (1992) by the Brahminical forces.

Why the victims of Brahminism are so indifferent? This is because our people simply can't understand the importance of the media.

As a journalist having spent 50 years in the field, I can tell you with full responsibility that except the Brahmin none in the country understands the importance of media. That is why not one speaker during this seminar referred to the need for our own media.

Cultural deprivation

Why the Bahujans (Scheduled Castes/Scheduled Tribes/ Backward Castes and Muslim/Christian/Sikhs) are not able to understand the importance of the media? This is an important question on which I have done good lot of pondering and come to the conclusion that Bahujans have become an unthinking lot because they have been culturally crushed, deprived, intellectually impoverished. Culture jamming is the most serious punishment, more serious than the death sentence. Cultural deprivation is living death. How can a culturally deprived people think of a media?

But remember, no battle against Brahminism is possible without our own media. Brahminism, every time, wins the battle because it has its own powerful media. And we have none.

Among the different weapons I am listing today to fight

Brahminism, I have given the highest priority to our own media.

We started the *Dalit Voice* with this objective and today it has become the oldest and the largest circulated journal of the oppressed Bahujans — all victims of Brahminism. *Dalit Voice* may be small and weak. But the bosses of Brahminism have given us the certificate that the blows inflicted on Brahminism by DV have been sufficiently hurtful. ∎

CHAPTER - III

Need for smaller states

Having touched the media, I will go into other subjects to diagnose the disease of Brahminism and after having diagnosed it, supply you the cheapest and the locally available medicine to cure the disease.

If you look at the different states of India, we find hardly any Brahmin chief minister except in the marxist-controlled West Bengal — where Brahmins deceived the people in the name of marxism. Brahmins, Baidyas and Kayasths — the three tiny *Bhadralok* upper castes — used marxism to further tighten their casteist-racist rule. West Bengal and Kerala are the standing examples.

It is only in Delhi —Union Government — we have a Brahmin Prime Minister. All the states have come into the hands of non-Brahmins. South India is a strong fortress against Brahmins. Maharashtra lately has a Dalit chief minister. If Vidarbha, Telengana, Harit Pradesh, Gorkhaland, Saurashtra are formed, power will flow down further and the Brahmin power will further shrink.

Brahmin has never been a leader. He is only a "leader" of leaders. Who will elect a Brahmin? As vote is entirely caste-based, the Brahmin who has no strength of population can never hold an elected post. So, the best weapon to strike at the Brahmin is by creating smaller and still smaller states to strengthen India's unity and integrity.

In Karnataka, I recommend the separation of Old Mysore from the Lingayat-dominated North Karnataka. The Vokkaligas fearing the Lingayat over-lordship had opposed the formation of Karnataka. But the Lingayats with the help of Brahmins deceived the Vokkaligas and formed Karnataka and then installed a Lingayat (S. Nijalingappa) as its first Chief Minister. The *Agni* paper must campaign for such a division of Karnataka.

Smaller the area of administration, better it is. Small is beautiful.

All those who are fighting against Brahminism must bear this in mind. *Akhand Bharat* is a *vaidik* slogan. It was once the sole aim of their organisation, RSS. They want a "united India" because larger the area of administration, Brahminism can have a better hold. The caste, language, regional and religious diversity of India is helpful for such a breakup of the country. The Brahminical forces are themselves helping this process towards decentralisation. The vote politics (electoral process) is hastening such a movement. Caste-based parties and their popularity indicate that a people belonging to a caste find better justice inside their own party. This is because each caste is a nation within the nation.

Bigger states like the UP, MP, Bihar have to be divided on ethnic lines. We have to start a movement in each area. In Europe, we have many countries which are smaller than a state inside India. ∎

✳ ✳ ✳

CHAPTER - IV

Who is a Brahmin?

Nobody spoke at the seminar on the special characteristics of the Brahmin. The Brahmin is so unique that nobody else in India enjoys such a special character. That is, Brahmin is one who must be a Brahmin by birth.

I can't become a Brahmin. You can't become a Brahmin. But you can become a Muslim, Christian or Sikh.

A Brahmin is the one who must be born to a Brahmin father. The mother is not important. The Brahmins (with the exception of another micro-minority community called Parsees belonging to the Zorastrian religion) are the only the people in the world who possess this special characteristic. You see those White American Krishna Consciousness fellows (ISKCON) jumping like monkeys, displaying their cross-thread. They are not Brahmins. Many others also display the "sacred thread". This 10-paisa thread is no passport to Brahminhood. A Brahmin is one who must be a born Brahmin. All those idiotic White Western Christians claiming to be Brahmins are given only the *shudra* status.

The only other people in the world who possess a similar characteristic are the Jews. Brahmins indeed are the "Jews of India". Both have identical characteristics. I have devoted a chapter itself to this subject in my book, *Brahminism* (DSA-2002).

Just as the 3% Brahmins are ruling India, the 3% Jews are ruling America. The two racial brothers have joined hands today. Brahmins have now become a powerful force with international connections. How to destroy Brahminism which today has become a world force? In the past three days, no speaker has said that it is possible to destroy Brahminism. I will not be wrong if I say that the conclusion of the seminar is that it is not possible to destroy Brahminism.

Remember: Brahminism never faced a single defeat in history after it destroyed Budhism. Ever since then it had a smooth ride. Not only it swallowed every other protest movement against Brahminism —like Veerashaivism, Periyar E.V. Ramaswamy's Dravida Kazagham — but it is now Brahminising Sikhism, Christianity. Even the revolutionary Islam is shaking inside India.

Such is the helplessness and incapacity of the victims of Brahminism. In fact, there is not even a public discussion on the havoc of Brahminism. This seminar is the first seminar of its kind in the whole of India. No victim of Brahminism has the courage to discuss the subject. We have no strategy and tactics to fight Brahminism. No doubt, we all hate Brahminism but we have no medicine to kill this pest. You may have a powerful, a very superior philosophy, far excelling Brahminism. But a mere philosophy cannot kill the enemy.

Strategies and tactics are as important as the philosophy. Sometimes, they are more important than the philosophy itself. Brahminism is not a philosophy. It is neither a philosophy nor a religion. Yet it is surviving solely because of its superior, unbeatable strategies and tactics. So, I want to devote some time to outline the different strategies and tactics to fight Brahminism. I am listing only the most important strategies and tactics which have been tried and tested during the past 30 years of our working experience. The Brahmins themselves have given us the certificate and admitted the efficacy of our strategies and tactics. The blow inflicted on Brahminism in the course of our 25 years of work has had its effect. We can make out from its groan and the grief. ∎

✳ ✳ ✳

CHAPTER - V

Law of Contradiction

Brahminical people thrive only by becoming experts in the Law of Contradictions. Their Vedas and all other "sacred scriptures" are a big bundle of contradictions. Arun Shourie, the Punjabi Brahmin, himself has admitted this in his book, *Hinduism: Essence & Consequence* (Vikas Publishing House, New Delhi, 1979).

Without studying this Law of Contradictions, we cannot even touch Brahminism, let alone defeating it.

What is this Law of Contradictions? I have gained expertise in this law which I studied from the writings of Mao Tse-tung. Every Brahmin is an expert on "contradictions". Because his "sacred scriptures" have made him a bundle of contradictions. If you have to defeat him in his game, you have to outsmart him in this game.

How every *Dalit Voice* prediction proved right

Those interested can read and study the Law of Contradictions of Mao. We will supply photo-copies of the book (pages 80). A study of this Law will give you a deadly weapon to destroy Brahminism.

The Law of Contradictions forms chapter -1 of the *Selected Works of Mao Tse-tung*. But I have with me a pocket book of this Chapter (Foreign Languages Press, Peking, 1968) presented to me when I visited Beijing.

The Law of Contradictions should not be mistaken as part of marxism just because it is written by Mao. The Law of Contradictions in things, that is, the law of the unity of the opposites, is the fundamental law of nature and of society and therefore also the fundamental law of thought. Every person who wants to get into public life will have to study this law. If not, the person will land in confusion and the forces that are opposed to the person will finish the person. Therefore, this law represents a great revolution in the history of human knowledge. The marxists used this knowledge in their materialist dialectics.

In the past 23 years we have been running the *Dalit Voice* (DV) journal and have met with hundreds of contradictions in our daily working. We have easily and effortlessly overcome all the contradictions because we have mastered this law. I keep this pocket book always on my study table and often read and re-read the book. Many members of the DV family have asked us how every prediction made in the DV has proved correct and how every complicated crisis we tackled was easily solved. The answer is our mastery over the Law of Contradictions.

The clash of opposites

It is very necessary that this tiny book of the Law of Contradictions has to be re-written adapting it to our peculiar and complex Indian conditions so that our Bahujan victims fighting Brahminism may find a ready reference.

To repeat: the Law represents a great revolution in the history of human knowledge. Contradiction is present in all process of objectively existing things and of subjective thought and permeates all these processes from beginning to end.

Please note: changelessness is the essence of Brahminical philosophy. They say misery, exploitation, slavery, pain have been existing all through history and these cannot be changed.

Those wanting to fight Brahminism have to go for the opposite and lay stress on change, more change and frequent changes.

Development comes out of the clash of contradictions inside a thing. The fundamental cause of the development of a thing is not external but internal. It lies in the contradictions within the thing. Contradictoriness within a thing is the fundamental cause of its development.

Changes in society are due chiefly to the development of the internal contradictions in society. The Brahminical people oppose and discourage internal contradictions. They want peace, tranquility, status quo. They don't want to stir the stinking pond that is India. But it is only by stirring up the dirty water and making it flow, the water gets purified and drinkable.

So, we, the victims of Brahminism, must always encourage clash of ideas, clash of classes and castes. If there had been no sharpening of the contradictions, the Congress, the original Brahminical party of India, would not have died.

Hate what the enemy loves

Contradictions between the old and the new, productive and non-productive forces, upper and lower castes, urban and rural, rich and the poor, landlord and the landless, factory-owner and the worker, bourgeoisie and the proletariat, old and new – these are some of the contradictions which have to be encouraged.

The Blacks in America fought the White rulers and today they are a power to be reckoned with. This happened also in South Africa where the Blacks overthrew the White Apartheid regime.

Struggle, fight, crisis — these are all part of life. Progress of a society depends entirely on the clash between these contradictions. No person or society interested in status quo likes such a clash of contradictions because the clash disturbs the society. Hate what the enemy loves and love what the enemy hates. Beautiful. This is the essence of the Law of Contradictions.

Internal revolution many a time is more important than external changes. This is true of an individual's body and the society also. It is through internal causes that external causes become operative.

Only after a thorough and a perfect study of the Law of Contradictions a person can lead a revolution. Or else he can't. The enemy will make you slip and you end up in frustration.

The Brahminical society in which we live is a bundle of contradictions that can confuse any ordinary person. Those fighting Brahminism have to be extraordinary persons with great knowledge of history, a perfect peep into the society with its myriad contradictions, and possess spotless, sterling character and integrity, a desciplined life. A slight slip in one thing is enough to fall into the trap.

Contradictions in Dr. R.M. Lohia

The *vaidik* is an extraordinary animal, cunning and crafty — a master crook. He watches you with a magnifying glass to find out your weaknesses — meaning any contradictions within you. And if he finds one contradiction in you, he will go on brain-washing you only on this contradiction and keep you fully preoccupied in meeting this one particular contradiction. And in doing so, you forget the rest of the contradictions and your time is over. You are dead.

That is why those interested in fighting Brahminism – a bundle of contradictions — should not suffer from even a single contradiction. You are finished.

Take the case of Dr. R.M. Lohia. He undoubtedly ranks third among India's greatest revolutionaries after Dr. Babasaheb Ambedkar and Periyar E.V. Ramaswamy. But he suffered from two main contradictions. His anti-English hatred and a deep dislike of marxism. No doubt, he was the father of the Backward Caste movement in the entire Hindi belt but the *vaidiks* who kept a strict vigil on him found out these two contradictions and pushed him deeper and deeper into crisis.

If you are a master of the Law of Contradictions, nobody can confuse you. Rather, you will confuse the Enemy. There is nothing in society that does not contain a contradiction. Without contradiction nothing will exist. Your greatness depends on the way you resolve this contradiction in a split second. Such an ability to solve the problem comes out of your deep knowledge of the Law of Contradictions.

In war, offence and defence, advance and retreat, victory and defeat — all are mutually contradictory phenomena. One cannot exist without the other.

Life itself is a struggle between contradictions. The society is full of contradictions. When you are in a revolutionary movement, the contradictions will be too many. You will be able to quickly solve the baffling contradictions before you and come to right conclusion if you are a master of the Law of Contradictions.

I will give you one famous example. The Brahminical people through their monopoly media have generated so much of hatred against Mrs. Sonia Gandhi. Any weak mind will simply succumb to this propaganda.

I am not a supporter of M.K. Gandhi's Congress, the original Brahminical Party of India. The Congress is the cause of all our problems. Hence the question is not of the Congress but of Sonia Gandhi. When the Brahminical forces so forcefully and unanimously denounce her, what stand those opposed to Brahminism will have to take? Love what the enemy hates and use that contradiction (Sonia Gandhi) to your advantage. This is what the Law of Contradictions says.

Dalits as leaders of Indian revolution must make a deep study of this law. Also make a deep study of the Enemy. Only after a deep study, you can launch the struggle against the Enemy. Fortunately for Dalits, Dr. Babasaheb Ambedkar has done this job. There is no aspect of the Enemy he has not studied. Babasaheb was a man without any contradictions.

Study the Enemy, study its literature, study the Hindu society, study the bundle of contradictions in the Hindu society. This should be our first duty.

Defects of Muslims

The Muslims may be born enemies of Brahminism because Islam is just the opposite of Brahminism. The two are like mongoose and serpent. Brahminism worships cow, Islam says cut the cow and eat it. Islam stands for no idol worship. Brahminism is only idol worship.

Islam being an egalitarian religion has become poison to Brahminism. That is why Brahminical people have manufactured thousands of stories to malign the Muslims. And those who have not studied Islam and Muslims will fall flat and their mind gets prejudiced against Islam.

Just because the religion of Islam is juxtaposed to Brahminism that does not mean the Muslims of India can fight Brahminism. They simply cannot fight Brahminism. And the Brahmins know it. They have made a deep study of Islam and the Indian Muslims.

Muslims of India know only who is their Enemy. That is all. But they have not made a study of this Enemy. Their *madrasas* do not teach Indian history and social sciences which are very important to prepare them for a fight. Many Muslims do not even know that the *vaidiks* are their oppressors. They are ignorant of the Brahminical tricks. They get quickly confused. (DV June 16, 2002 p. 6: "*Madrasa syllabus must include social science & history*", Ilyas Patel).That is why Muslims are failing to fight the Enemy. (Rajendra: *Muslim Failure to See Through Brahminical Tricks — A Dalit Viewpoint*, DSA-2002, Rs. 5).

Even while dealing with different contradictions, you cannot treat all the contradictions equally. There are major contradictions, minor contradictions, non-antagonistic contradictions, fundamental contradictions, principal contradiction, temporary contradiction etc. There are varieties of contradictions. All contradictions cannot be treated equally. Each is different and each needs different treatment depending upon its time, place and situation.

Dalit-Backward Caste contradiction

I will give one more example. Brahminical people are encouraging and grooming some Dalit writers, funding them and giving them wide publicity in their papers, to mislead the Dalits and say the Brahmin is not our enemy but the Backward Castes. (DV June 1, 2002 p.5: "*Brahmin writer manufactures a new enemy for Dalits*"). Did Dr. Babasaheb Ambedkar, who is our final authority on this subject, say this? No.

It is true the Backward Castes (BCs) persecute Dalits in rural India. Yes. There is a contradiction between the Scheduled Castes (SCs) and BCs. This is well reflected in the antagonism between Mayawati and Mulayam Singh Yadav in UP. But Mayawati is heading a party called the Bahujan Samaj which includes the BCs. If the SCs start identifying BCs as the enemy then there will be no Bahujan Samaj. BCs no doubt are a contradiction but they are a minor contradiction. (DV Aug.16, 2003 p.18, V.T.Rajshekar: *"Dalit-Brahmin unity is against science of society & violates edict of Dr. Ambedkar"*).

Those Dalits interested in fighting Brahminism will be bogged down, their attention diverted and made to waste all their time and finally destroyed in fighting this minor contradiction.

Principal contradiction

Backward Castes no doubt are a contradiction which has to be fought. There is no difference of opinion on this. But their turn will come only after we fight and eliminate the principal contradiction which we have to identify and then fight. The principal contradiction in India is Brahminism — not the BCs.

Resolving a contradiction means to take a quick decision, answer a question, settle a dispute, handle a given work or direct an operation. One who is able to resolve any contradiction means one who will have no confusion in arriving at the right conclusion.

At a given time we are confronted with numerous contradictions. Of this some contradictions get intensified and some are temporarily resolved. At this stage some new ones suddenly crop up. It is at such complex situations a deep study of the Law Contradictions will help us.

Look at the Hindu nazi party. They have a *Swadeshi* wing which wants to encourage everything made in India and boycott or destroy everything made outside India. But the Hindu nazi party (RSS) is the party of our upper caste rulers (Hindus) who have their heart in America. They love everything West. They speak their language (English) and flaunt everything made in the West. They like foreign perfume, foreign cars, foreign kerchief and even foreign wife. Scotch whisky. How to reconcile this baffling behaviour of the Hindu with the *swadeshi* stand of their nazi party? Ordinary fellows will get confused. The Brahminical forces thrive on confusing us. Prime Minister Vajpayee eats beef but his party is against cow slaughter. He talks *swadeshi* but drinks *videshi*. His Education Minister wants education in Sanskrit but Brahmins have totally forgotten Sanskrit and have switched over to English. The Sanskrit *patashalas* are today educating non-Brahmin students.

Brahminism will suddenly confront us with such baffling contradictions and throw us into serious confusion, and we will get lost. The Law of Contradictions will help us out.

How DV makes correct predictions

Life itself is full of contradictions. Development itself is due to play of contradictions. In such a situation, we should have the ability to identify the principal contradiction which influences all other contradictions. In a country like India with its myriad castes, classes, communities, religions, languages, regions etc., the relationship between the principal contradiction and non-principal contradictions will confront us with a mind-boggling problem. Ordinary person will be simply confused. And Brahminism survives only by confusing us.

The Law of Contradictions will teach us that at every stage of development of a process, there will be only one principal contradiction which plays the leading role. Once we master the Law of Contradictions, we can easily identify the principal contradiction and resolve it with ease. That is how in DV we always arrive at the right conclusion and are able to make correct forecasts.

When there are two or more contradictions, we must make

every effort to identify the principal contradiction. Once this principal contradiction is identified and understood, all other minor contradictions can be easily resolved.

The one and the only principal contradiction in India is Brahminism. I will give you an example. Brahminical forces are doing everything to impress upon Dalits that the BCs are our real enemy (principal contradiction) and then divert our mind, time and energy to fight the BCs. Our Dalit activists and writers get confused and commit all sorts of mistakes and then get deceived. Brahminical forces also tell us that our enemy is the Muslim. Our enemy is doing everything to confuse us. Because it has its monopoly media to confuse us. It is the Enemy's job to confuse us. But it is our job not to get confused. Neither the BCs nor the Muslims are our Enemy. It is Brahminism which has to be fought and finished first.

So, Brahminism is the principal contradiction. All other contradictions are secondary. Once the principal contradiction is eliminated all other minor or non-antagonistic contradictions like the BCs or Muslims will vanish.

Terrorism is the other word for Muslims

Brahminism also deceives us by saying "terrorism" (read Muslim) is the main enemy of the society. They succeeded in diverting our attention and then deceiving us during the Mandal Commission agitation (1991) and consuming our time and energy against Muslims by placing before us an imaginary problem (contradiction) of Babri Masjid. Both the BCs, the beneficiaries of Mandal Commission report, and Dalits who spearheaded the Mandal agitation, fell flat before the Brahminical treachery and got deceived.

The principal contradiction in India, therefore, is Brahminism. All other minor and unimportant contradictions will be automatically resolved once this principal contradiction is eliminated. A proper study of the Law of Contradictions will teach us all this and will make us masters of the situation and defeat the cunning forces.

There are thousands of scholars among SC/ST/BCs and Muslim/Christian/Sikhs but we are sorry to say they have not made a study of this Law. They have not even heard of such a Law.

If two contradictions are suddenly placed before us, we must have the ability to quickly judge which is the principal and which is the secondary contradiction. Both can't be treated equally.

Every Brahmin is an expert in the Law of Contradictions because all his "sacred scriptures" are a bundle of contradictions. And hence by studying them he has become an expert in this law. Muslims, Christians and Sikhs are not as much confused as Dalits and BCs. Their religions have given them a better grounding. But the SC/ST/BCs having been totally *hinduised* (enslaved) they simply collapse and fall a prey to Brahminical machinations.

Dr. Ambedkar proves right

In a given situation or time **A** is the principal contradiction, and **B** is the non-principal contradiction. At another given situation or time, **A** may take the place of **B** and vice-versa or a new contradiction may crop up.

M.K. Gandhi supported by Brahminism asked the people of India to launch a "freedom struggle" against the British to establish an "independent India". Dr. Babasaheb Ambedkar differed from Gandhi. He said the Untouchables were persecuted not by the British but the Brahminical forces.

Gandhi and Dr. Ambedkar each presented a different principal contradiction but Babasaheb's judgement was right. History has proved him right.

The Law of Contradictions will also help us to decide the nature of our struggle in India. Brahminism is a socio-cultural fascist force. It is not an economic force. Nor is it a political force. Brahminism first attained political power and then economic power after decades of socio-cultural counter-revolution. RSS was established only in the year 1925. But the Brahminical revivalism began with the destruction of Budhism by Adi Shankara centuries ago. Since then came a number of Hindu socio-cultural-religious leaders to revive Brahminism. Dayananda Saraswati, B.G. Tilak, Raja Rammohan Roy, Aurobindo, Vivekananda, Lala Lajpat Rai, M.K. Gandhi to name the prominent ones. None of these people worked for any political power for Brahmins. Their attention was fully pre-occupied with Brahminical socio-cultural revivalism.

Demolishing superstructure

Gandhi confused the masses of India and conferred the greatest benefits on Brahminism by defeating Dr. Ambedkar through the "Poona Pact" and then diverting the attention of the country to "driving the British out". He installed the first Brahmin Prime Minister (Jawahar Lal Nehru) on "independent" India. Even after that the RSS and other Brahminical forces did not work for political power. They were confining themselves to building up their socio-cultural hold on the masses (*hinduising* the SC/ST/BCs). Even as this is written the BJP, their political party, is not ruling India. It is a coalition government headed by a BJP Prime Minister.

Brahminism came to the centre stage only a couple of years back. It is now taking an aggressive, violent posture after decades of socio-cultural revivalist struggle. That is why Dr. Ambedkar called for a thorough-going socio-cultural revolution before trying to capture power through vote politics.

When the superstructure of the society — namely its social, cultural, educational, judicial, financial, bureaucratic, media and political setup — is completely with Brahminism, how can we the persecuted slaves capture political power? It is a pipe dream. So, all revolutionary sections have to first demolish this superstructure through a thoroughgoing socio-cultural revolution. This is the Law of Contradiction.

Place of antagonism

Brahminical people are Aryans and hence foreigners. This is not our claim. It is the claim made by the Brahmins only. The SC/ST/BCs are indigenous and children of this soil. Antagonism between the two, therefore, is natural. But have not the Brahminical people and the SC/ST/BCs, who are persecuted by them, been existing together for a long time? For centuries? Even today they are existing together.

How two antagonistic forces can exist together? This is because no contradiction has developed between the two to a certain stage to assume the form of open hostility, clash and finally revolution.

Brahmins are about 3% — a minuscule minority. But they have assumed the power to think on behalf of the entire Hindu society. They know that if they allow the contradictions between the two sections to be sharpened, the antagonism will reach such an explosive stage that the very life of the Brahmin will be in danger. He knows it. That is why he is using all the power of the media, temples, myth-making, Sanskrit, re-writing of history to direct our anger against the non-antagonistic Muslims and Christians. Lately, he is using the state power itself to see that the contradictions do not get sharpened.

The SC/ST/BCs including Muslim/Christians/Sikhs (the Bahujans) must know that the contradiction between us and Brahminism is bound to be there. And unless this contradiction is sharpened and made to explode into a revolutionary war which results in the overthrow of the Brahminical rulers, there can be no progress in the society. Contradiction, clash and war between two opposite sections is inevitable and unavoidable. This is the Law of the Contradictions.

Gandhi, a counter-revolutionary

There are some do-gooders among us who come to advice us saying "Are there no good Brahmins? Why blame Brahmins alone?" To such do-gooders our reply is to read history. We have no quarrel with any individual Brahmin. Our fight is against a system that is oppressing us. Brahmins themselves are victims of Brahminism. They have to be saved. Hence Bahujans have to be on one side and Brahminism on the opposite side. The clash between the two is inevitable. This clash can be only postponed but it can never be avoided. Social revolution is not only entirely necessary but also entirely practicable. This is the message given to us by all the greatest revolutionaries of India: Budha, Mahatma Phule, Guru Nanak, Sri Narayana Guru, Babasaheb Ambedkar, Periyar E.V. Ramaswamy etc.

M.K. Gandhi was a counter-revolutionary. He misled the oppressed masses and deceived them and destroyed the revolution.

Contradiction and struggle are universal, absolute. But the form of struggle may differ according to different circumstances.

This is the greatness of the Law of Contradictions and the absolute necessity of its scientific study in India which is a land of extreme contradictions.

The Brahmins, who are experts on this Law, play upon the different contradictions in society and we the ignorant fellows fall a prey and get further enslaved.

I have sat through the 3-day seminar. I did not find a single speaker who was not critical of Brahminism. Every speaker and every member in the audience was against Brahminism.

That means, Dalits, BCs, Vokkaligas, Lingayats —all those who spoke — were all against Brahminism. Over 90% of Indians hate Brahminism. If this is a fact, why they are not able to touch Brahminism? This is because they have not studied the Law of Contradictions. Nay. They have not even heard of this Law. Many things are kept a top secret in this country. The Law of Contradictions is one such.

Are BCs enemy of Dalits ?

This Law tells us the difference between minor contradiction, major contradiction, antagonistic and non-antagonistic contradiction and the principal contradiction.

I will give one example of a meeting called by the Editor of *Agni*, Sridhar, on holding a cultural event here in Bangalore. I was also present. At this meeting some Dalit representatives expressed reservations about supporting the proposed cultural event because it was not an exclusive Dalit event. They had some reservation regarding the participation of some BC writers. It is true the Dalits in rural areas are victims of BC violence. This makes the Dalits to think the BCs as the Enemy No.1 of Dalits. Brahminical people through their media also fan such a BC-SC clash and conflict. Divide and rule is the secret of Brahmin rulership. The Brahminical rulers are financing some Dalit writers to sharpen the SC-BC contradictions.

We mistake a minor or a non-antagonistic contradiction as the principal contradiction. This is the problem with all critics of Brahminism. This is the cause of our failure to offer a fight to Brahminism despite all our awful population strength.

Finish the principal enemy first. Who is the principal enemy? Finding this is our main task. Fight this principal enemy first. A study of the Law of Contradictions will help us to find the badly needed deadly weapon to destroy Brahminism.

Love what the enemy hates

What is this weapon? The first weapon is: Love what the Enemy hates and hate what the enemy loves. This is contradiction.

If this one lesson is mastered, Brahminism can be beaten to pulp and made half dead. DV has mastered this law and tested it. I am telling you out of my experience.

Vivekananda & *Upanishads*

Prof. K.S. Bhagavan, a noted honest intellectual, in his speech criticised Brahminism but praised *Upanishads* and Vivekananda. Here is a contradiction in his thought. Did the Brahmins reject Vivekananda and the *Upanishads*? No. It may be true that all the *Upanishads* are written by the Kshatriyas and non-Brahmins. Vivekananda may be also called a great *Vedantist*. It is true that Vivekananda was a Bengali (shudra) Kayasth. But just because the *Upanishads* are products of non-Brahmins and Vivekananda was non-Brahmin, did the Brahmins reject them? No. Prof. Bhagavan is sincere in his fight against Brahminism. But in his speech he confessed his helplessness. He admitted that Brahminism cannot be destroyed. This is because of his failure to study the Law of Contradictions.

Arun Shourie in his book, *Hinduism: Essence and Consequence,* has torn the *Upanishads* to pieces. But angry Brahmins rejected this book and later forced withdrawal of the book itself from circulation. Vikas, its famous publishers, have refused to reprint the book fearing the Brahmin wrath.

Our point is the Brahmins do not hate the *Upanishads*. Rather, they consider it sacred because it serves their interests. ■

✳ ✳ ✳

CHAPTER - VI

Beef-eating

I had suggested to Fr. Albert and Brother Chand Peer of the Indian Social Institute, Bangalore (where this seminar was held), to serve beef for lunch on the last day. But they disappointed us. I find some Brahminism among the Jesuits who run this institution. Beef-eating is a deadly weapon to destroy Brahminism. It will sharpen the contradictions.

In Cubbon Park, Bangalore , I had arranged one such beef party over 23 years ago right before the Vidhana Soudha, the seat of the State Government. The Brahmins were then shocked. It is not possible to arrange such a beef party in public today in Bangalore or any other city of India. The Brahmins will engineer a riot and force the state itself to book you. Brahminism has grown to enormous size in the past 20 years.

But beef-eating is a deadly weapon that can inflict a fatal blow on Brahminism. Every Dalit and critic of Brahminism must eat beef and proudly announce he is a beef-eater. The very central nerve in the Brahminical brain will break down on hearing that you are a beef-eater. I refuse to attend any Budhist conversion ceremony unless beef is served for lunch.

Sikh surrender to Brahminism

Look at the Sikhs. In 1984, under the leadership of Sant Bhindranwale they fought a bloody battle against Brahminism. A couple of years before this I had a meeting with the Sant and cautioned him that the battle against Brahminism was not physical but intellectual. Brahmins being just 3%, the brave Sikhs would have no problem to achieve self-determination for Sikhs in Punjab if they had employed right strategies and tactics. The one deadly weapon I suggested to the Sant was that he should give a call to Sikhs to eat beef for which there was no scriptural prohibition under Sikhism. I had suggested many other intellectual steps. But he did not heed my words but took to physical fight. And the Brahminical rulers used the state power itself (Army) and crushed the Sikh struggle in what became famous as "Blue Star Operation". Thousands and thousands of brave Sikh men, women and children died in the Golden Temple, Amritsar, itself. Today, the Sikhs have totally surrendered to Brahminism and their main Sikh party (Akali Dal) has an alliance with the Hindu nazi party. One simple remedy of beef-eating would have achieved all the miracles without a single drop of blood.

Today, the ban on cow slaughter is on the top of the ruling Brahminical party agenda. From this we can make out the importance they attach to cow. Because they know by banning beef-eating they can enlsave both Muslims and Dalits — both beef-eaters. If you want to fight Brahminism not only all beef-eaters must unite but publicly arrange beef-parties. Brahminism will be half dead. ■

CHAPTER - VII

Reject Gandhi & Gandhism

M.K. Gandhi might have been killed by a Brahmin but Gandhi and Gandhism are loved and propagated mainly by Brahmins. This is the contradiction in Brahminism. Brahmins hate Gandhi. Even today on the day Gandhi was killed (Jan.31), the mother party of Brahmins, RSS, distributes sweets. But it is the Brahmins who carry this Gujarati Bania on their heads and pounce upon you like a mad dog whenever Gandhi is criticised.

One of the deadly weapons to kill Brahminism is to reject Gandhi and his Gandhism. Because Gandhism is the more colourful and deceptive mask of Brahminism.

So, reject Gandhi and kill Gandhism. Killing Gandhism is as good as killing Brahminism. Please read the following books for a deeper study of this subject:-

1. Dr. B.R. Ambedkar, *What Congress & Gandhi have done to Untouchables*, Thacker & Co., 1945. (Vol.9, *Dr. Babasaheb Ambedkar Writings & Speeches*, 1991, Maharashtra Govt. Press, Marine Drive, Bombay - 400 004).

2. V.T. Rajshekar, *Why Godse Killed Gandhi?*, DSA-1997

3. Dr. Velu Annamalai, *Sergeant-Major M.K. Gandhi*, DSA-1995

4. Fazlul Huq, *Gandhi: Saint or Sinner?*, DSA-1991

5. V.T. Rajshekar, *Hinduism, Fascism & Gandhism*, DSA-1985.

Unity with Muslims

Brahminical people hate Muslims and Islam because Islam stands for justice, equality, brotherhood and no idol worship. Brahminism represents just the opposite. If you want to kill Brahminism, then we have to seek unity with Muslims. Love what the Enemy hates. Simple.

M.N. Roy, country's leading marxist and a Bengali Brahmin, has said in his book, *Historical Role of Islam*, (1981, Ajanta Books, Jawahar Nagar, Delhi - 110 007), that Islam is the best weapon to destroy Brahminism.

Periyar E.V. Ramaswamy, another bitterest foe of Brahmins, has called upon *shudras* to embrace Islam to escape Hindu slavery. (Periyar E.V. Ramaswamy: *Salvation to Shudra Slavery*, DSA-1986).

Stop this "Hindu-Muslim unity" business. This is nonsense. "Hindu-Muslim unity" is never possible. What is possible is Dalit-Muslim unity. (Dr. Ram Nath, *Dalit-Muslim Unity, Why & How?*, DSA-1995). ■

✳   ✳   ✳

CHAPTER - VIII

"Socialist Brahmins"

During the seminar, I found some speakers criticising Brahminism but at the same time suggesting "united action" with "progressive or liberal" Brahmins. Brahminism and "progressive thinking" do not go together. One is contradictory to the other. There is nothing like a "progressive Brahmin" or a "liberal Brahmin". Medha Patkar, Swami Agnivesh, Ramakrishna Hegde, Justice V.R. Krishna Iyer, E.M.S. Namboodiripad, etc. are more dangerous because they put on a mask of socialism or liberalism to deceive us.

The sole objective of these "liberal Brahmins" is to catch all those people fighting Brahminism, mislead them and misdirect them and thereby help their *jatwalas*. Beware of "Socialist Brahmins".

Togadia, Narendra Modi, Uma Bharati, even L.K. Advani are our best friends. They don't hide their hatred against us. They openly criticise and also kill Muslims, Dalits, Christians etc. We have no difficulty in identifying Bal Thackeray as our Enemy. Because he is our honest enemy.

I have written a book itself on this subject, *Dialogue of the Bhoodevatas* (Socialist Brahmins vs. Sacred Brahmins, DSA-1993). It was translated to Urdu and other languages. But I am sorry to tell you that the only people who read this book and fully understood it are the Brahmins. The book is no doubt sold out but I am sorry to say that there was never a debate on this important book in DV.

This book is essentially devoted to one aspect of the Law of Contradictions in which every Brahmin is an expert. We may be critical of the Brahmin and their Brahminism but I have to admit with sorrow that we the victims of Brahminism are not a sharp people. There is a kink in our brains. Dr. Ambedkar himself had said this with great sorrow. We have filled our brains with so much of Brahminical shit that it does not allow us to come to a right conclusion. That is why all these "Socialist Brahmins" like Gandhi, Jayaprakash Narayan, Vinoba Bhave, Ramakrishna Hegde, Medha Patkar, V.R. Krishna Iyer attract our people and get deceived.

Never admit a *vaidik*

Budhism suffered because Budha admitted the Brahmins into his *Sangha*. This was a great mistake. Look at the Brahmins, they will never admit you into their inner circles. In all temples, you are asked to remove your shirt to check if you have the thread. If you have no thread, you have a separate entrance. No non-Brahmin is so far made a Shankarachari. No non-Brahmin was made chief of the RSS except once for a very brief period. We may be critical of the Brahmin but we have to learn a lot of things from them. For love of one's *jati*, you have to learn from the Brahmins.

That doesn't mean we have anything against the Brahmins. Look at our village system which even to this day is in tact from centuries. Brahmins rarely live in a village and even if there is one, they live in total seclusion. The Untouchables live outside the village because of the social segregation (racism) enforced by Brahminism. The Untouchables may resent this racism but they don't forcibly enter and trouble the Brahmins. The Dalits don't interfere with the Brahmins or other upper castes and their lives.

When we don't interfere with Brahmins either in villages or cities, why should the Brahmins come to us and meddle in our affairs? The Brahminical people have set up their communist, socialist parties, naxalite outfits, human rights forums to meddle with our lives. Lately, thousands of NGOs have sprung up all headed by the upper castes. Many NGOs have "fallen in love" with Dalits. In the name of Dalits, they are flourishing. In the tribal areas, the Brahminical menace is too much. The Pejawara Swami is going into "*Harijan* colonies" and constructing temples. All sorts of nuisance. Why should these people meddle with our lives when we don't trouble them? Is there one instance in India where we have infiltrated their ranks? The couple of "*Harijan* temple entry" stunts are again stage-managed by the upper castes. Untouchables are not Hindu and were never Hindu. Our people are not interested in temple entry. They are fighting for justice, self-respect. When that is the case, the Brahminical people should stop interfering with the lives of our people when we don't interfere with their lives. "You allow us to lead our lives". This is our request to Brahmins. It is in this sense, we call upon our people not to admit Brahmins into any of our organisations.

Brahmins are good servants but bad masters. Remember Periyar E.V. Ramaswamy's warning.

CHAPTER - IX

Language problem

Yet another serious contradiction by which Brahminism is killing us is by using the language to keep us divided and also enslaved. Kannada film actor Rajkumar has educated all his children in English schools but says he is ready to die for Kannada. Rajkumar may be a BC but he is a stooge of Brahminism which is using him to keep our people in mental slavery.

Brahmins and other upper castes talk even to their dogs in English. But tell us to eat in Kannada, sleep in Kannada, and finally die in Kannada. They educate their children only in English schools and become computer kids, go to America, make millions and then come back as "experts" and rule us.

But we the victims of Brahminism study only in Kannada and become clerks and peons — good servants. Slaves enjoying their slavery.

This blind love of Kannada (this applies all the Indian languages) has made us hate English but Brahmins master English and become our bosses and reach international heights. This is the case in all the states of India. Look at Bombay city, the capital of Maharashtra. Non-Maharashtrian upper castes are controlling its business, media, cinema etc. Maharashtrians have become good servants because they became victims of the Brahminical language policy.

Earlier, the Brahmins defeated us by denying Sanskrit education. And today after "independence", they again defeated us by denying the English education. Today, they are ready to teach us Sanskrit, a dead language, which has no market. Language is a deadly weapon in the hands of Brahmins to defeat us. But our people, slaves, cannot see through this Brahminical game to keep us enslaved.

As Editor of DV, I am suffering like anything because of this language division among the victims of Brahminism. All over India, SC/ST/BCs have become good slaves because they don't know English. Nobody told them not to study English. But the Brahmins told them to hate English saying that English was a foreign language of the British. They told us that by using the English the British enslaved us. We believed the Brahmins but did not believe our own master, Dr.Babasaheb Ambedkar, who despite being an Untouchable was a master of English and attained international heights through English.

I am telling you: You can't fight Brahminism unless you master the English language. This is no disrespect to our mother tongue. English today is the international language, accepted as such all over the world. If you reject English and stick to your mother tongue, it means you are allowing Brahminism to flourish. If you want to fight and defeat Brahminism, it is possible only if you master English along with your mother tongue. Dr. Ambedkar did it and demonstrated his power. Babasaheb's own children have eyes but can't see. They have ears but can't hear. Brahminism has made us blind and deaf. What a tragedy.

Yet another suggestion to fight Brahminism: We have to remove all Sanskrit words from our Indian languages. Tamil is India's only language which has not a single Sanskrit word. We have to follow this example. South Indians have to set an example in weeding out all the existing Sanskrit words and coining appropriate words. This is a big job but we have to do it. Brahminism will then start shivering. ∎

* * *

CHAPTER - X

Identity

This is a very important and also a very vast subject. I have so far given you seven major weapons to fight Brahminism. Now, I am giving youyet another important, perhaps the deadliest, weapon of ethnic **identity**.

What is going on today inside India is a fight between the indigenous Bahujans (SC/ST/BCs -65% and Muslims/Christians/Sikhs 20% —total 85%) and the alien Aryans (15%). The Brahmins (3%) are fanning the flames of hatred between the different sections of indigenous people and making them fight each other and then kill each other. Brahminism is dividing all the victims of Brahminism and then ruling us. The Brahmins are encouraging some Dalit writers and giving them a regular column in their daily papers to advocate that the real enemy of the Dalits is the BCs. This mischief will get more pronounced as days pass and the contradictions will get sharpened.

This 85% of the indigenous population — divided into hundreds of castes, subcastes, tribes, sects, ethnic units —wants to retain its **identity** but the Brahmins want to destroy this **identity**.

Before 1947 ("independence"), Brahminism tried to destroy us by launching a fake "freedom struggle" under the leadership of Gandhi. Our people joined Gandhi but did not go with Dr. Ambedkar. But when the Brahmins learnt that under "independent India", Muslims and Dalits would unite and finish Brahminism, they conspired to partition India. C. Rajagopalachari, called the "Southern Fox", was the brain behind this partition.

Come to Karnataka. We have three ruling castes: Lingayats, Vokkaligas and Brahmins. How did the three become rulers? They became rulers only by strengthening their ethnic **identity**. They strengthened their *jati* organisations, established their own religious mutts, priestly order, educational institutions, banks, cooperative societies and even a secret militia. After strengthening all these, they were able to capture political power. And political power was further used to strengthen their *jatis*. It is through their *jati* strength they came to power - not vice versa.

Take the neighbouring Andhra Pradesh where you have the Reddys and Khammas as rulers. In UP, Mayawati became Chief Minister by strengthening the **identity** of her Chamar *jati*.

Kerala example

Take Kerala, the rulers there are Brahmins, Nairs, Syrian Christians and Muslims. Though the Backward Caste Ezhavas form 30% of the population — single largest — it could not become the ruler because it did not strengthen its *jati*. Only those who strengthened their ethnic **identity** (*jati*) through a socio-cultural revolution became rulers. Brahmins are ruling the whole country right from "independence" only by following this time-tested principle.

After having developed their *jatis* through their mutts, gods, their own educational institutions, banks etc., the Brahmins are now telling our people to destroy our castes.

For this, they are quoting Dr. Ambedkar's book, *Annihilation of Caste,* and thereby misleading us. This book was written by Babasaheb not for our Bahujan castes but the Hindu castes. The SC/ST/BC castes are not "castes" but **ethnic identities**, kin groups. They are all the original inhabitants of India. Untouchables are outcastes, meaning outside the caste. Our "castes" are not part of the Hindu caste system. The caste system is the other name for Hinduism or *Chaturvarna* - which includes only four *varnas* —Brahmin, Kshatriya, Vaishya, Shudra. Only these four *varnas* have castes and subcastes. SC/ST/BCs are not part of this four-fold caste system. Our "castes" are our ethnic **identities**. They are kin groups. India had hundreds of different tribes. SC/ST/BC castes are all tribes. Our caste and subcaste names are our tribal names.

If each SC/ST/BC caste and subcaste strengthens its respective **identity**, it can also become rulers. The ruling upper castes have shown us the way. There is no other way but to follow this time-tested path. Take the case of Kurubas (shepherds) of Karnataka. It may be the single largest caste group under the BC list of the state. But it is still weak.

Pathetic case of Vokkaligas

How did Deve Gowda become the Chief Minister of Karnataka? All the Gowdas came to Bangalore with a stick and some stones in their pockets and threatened Deve Gowda's Brahmin rival, Ramakrishna Hegde. Four Brahmins were beaten up on that day of the election. Hegde was about to be beaten up but the police protected him. The Gowda muscle power made Deve Gowda Chief Minister. Later he became the Prime Minister.

But the Kurubas failed to get chief ministership because they did not bring sticks and stones to Bangalore. And that is how Siddaramaiah, the Kuruba candidate, failed to become the Chief Minister.

Vokkaligas have become weak. They cannot fight the Lingayats and Brahmins because they are losing their **identity**. Vokkaligas have become culturally weak because they are worshipping Brahmin gods, not their *desi* gods. (DV June 1, 2003 p.16:

"*Vokkaligas: Pathetic case of a jati destroying itself*"). I have given hundreds of examples on this question of **identity** in DV. We had a five-year-long debate in DV on the question of "*caste identity*". Finally I wrote a book itself on this subject: *Caste — A Nation Within the Nation* (Books for Change, Bangalore, 2002).

Take the case of Jagjivan Ram statue coming up in Bangalore before the Vidhana Soudha, the seat of the State Government. Jagjivan Ram is no comparison before the giant Babasaheb. Yet Ram is becoming increasingly popular because the neglected Chamars (Madigas) in South India and Maharashtra consider him their leader. He symbolises the rising Chamar power. This is "*caste identity*". You can't say the Chamars are wrong.

Do you know who is the greatest opponent and critic of my ethnic **identity** thesis? It is the Brahminical upper castes.

They have come to know the power of this deadly weapon. Why the Brahmins all over India hate my thesis? Because they are sharp enough to understand how deadly this thesis is to their existence. If the Law of Contradictions says "Love what the enemy hates", then we have to love the ethnic **identity** thesis. But do you know that my thesis is still opposed by some unthinking Dalits though their number is dwindling? They are not able to understand even this much.

Our people are not able to understand this thesis. They still talk of "Annihilation of Caste". The thesis is "use caste to kill the caste system". ■

Beauty of the broken mirror

Mogalli Ganesh, a Dalit Professor from Hampi University, in his paper has given a good example of a "broken mirror". According to him India was once like a huge mirror. The invading Aryans broke this huge mirror and each indigenous tribal unit is today holding on to a small piece of this mirror. This tiny piece of mirror is of different shape and different size. His question is: should we join all these tiny broken pieces or hold on to each broken piece?

My reply is India has been always a broken mirror. It was never one single huge mirror. It was only the British who made an attempt for the first time in history to join these broken pieces of mirror but did not succeed. Even when British India was one "united country", there were several hundred princely states which were outside this British empire. Hyderabad was the largest state outside the British empire. So also old Mysore. Also Kashmir and Travancore-Cochin. Did the people in those princely states outside die? In fact the development of SC/ST/BCs and Muslim/Christian/Sikhs was much better under princely rule.

Neither the Aryans broke the mirror of India nor the British tried to join it. Is it possible to join any broken mirror? Even if you join it with some quick-fix gum, the patched up mirror will continue to reflect hundreds of images of the face looking into that broken mirror.

What is wrong with a small piece of mirror? Every lady's handbag will have one such tiny mirror which is sufficient to meet her needs. Even this tiny pocket mirror is sufficient to see your face and do the make- up. People travelling in train don't carry a big mirror. They all manage with a tiny mirror. It meets their needs.

This tiny mirror represents each caste, subcaste or tribal unit which is a self-sufficient, self-satisfied ethnic unit.

It is the Brahminical forces who want to patch up all these broken mirrors and produce that elusive *Akhand Bharat* mirror. India is not a "nation" and was never a "nation". A broken mirror can never be joined. Each broken piece represents that basic building brick, our ethnic **identity** which is the best and the deadliest weapon to destroy Brahminism.

Brahminism wants to join all these broken pieces of mirror artificially, putting the cement of Hinduism. This is not possible. Nor it will be allowed.

The beauty of India is that it is a broken mirror. The Constitution of India calls it "Union of States". Any effort to cement this broken pieces into a huge mirror —called the "cultural nationalism", Hindutva, *Akhand Bharat* — is against nature, against humanity. India has to remain a big zoo with all types of animals, birds, fish, reptiles. The greatness of India is its dazzling ethnic diversity. It has to remain so. Then only it will retain its beauty. The beauty of India is it is one huge mirror of several broken pieces.

Caste-based political parties

Caste-based political parties are coming up all over India in a big way. Brahmins hate caste-based parties. They make fun of Mayawati, Laloo Prasad, Dr. Ramadoss, Mulayam Singh Yadav dubbing them casteist. But everything in India is selected or elected on the basis of caste. Caste-based parties are an extension of our "*caste identity*" thesis. Since India is not a "nation", national parties are dying. The future is for small, caste-based or region-based parties.

Caste is not dead. It will never be dead. It is alive and going strong. Every caste is alive. Bharatiya Janata Party is a party of Brahmins and Banias. There are parties for Jats, Khammas, Marathas, Nairs, Syrian Christians. It is good that each *jati* has its own party. We must encourage it.

Brahmins have already studied my *"caste identity"* book and refused to review it, refused to give it any publicity. Because they know the danger of my thesis.

Hence to fight Brahminism, we have to strengthen every caste and subcaste. Brahminism will be dead. Use caste to kill caste system (Brahminism).

Strengthen every caste

Pour some water on your hand. You can drink that water by holding all the fingers tight in the shape of a cup. The five fingers in your hand are different, one separate from the other. Once all the five fingers are united and held tight, it becomes a cup and helps you to drink that water. But withdraw one finger, the water is lost. What does it show? The Brahmins can drink the water when all your fingers in one hand are made into a cup. Withdraw one finger, the water is lost. Only when all the fingers (castes) are held tight, the Brahmins can drink the water. Each finger is like a caste or subcaste. Strengthen each caste and it will never cooperate and allow the Brahmin to drink the water from your hand. This is the kernel of the *"caste identity"* thesis.

The unanimous opinion of every speaker at the 3-day seminar was that it was not possible to destroy Brahminism or Hinduism. Once every *jati* is strengthened and gets its share in proportion to its population, what is wrong in remaining as Hindu?

Unity is the Brahmin slogan. As against this our slogan should be **separate but equal**.

The Brahminical forces often stress the need for "national unity" or "Hindu unity" because when all the fingers are united, the Brahmin can sip the water. Unity is, therefore, the slogan of the Brahminical people, our oppressors. Because they have no strength of numbers. It is the SC/ST/BCs and Muslim/ Christian/Sikhs who have the strength of numbers. We are over 85% but they (Hindus) are a mere 15%. To unite all the fingers (castes), so that it can be made into a cup to drink the water, the Brahmins are deceiving us by talking of "unity".

Sikh example

Yes. We are also for unity. But we have a different conception of unity. What we say is we are ready for such a unity only when we are recognised as **separate but equal**. The Brahmin is not ready to admit our separateness, admit our distinct **identity**. Nor he is ready to call us as his equals. When they are not ready for our terms, we can't agree for their call of unity.

When each caste or subcaste gets itself strengthened, then it will have the intellectual strength and also the strength of numbers to acquire property and positions in proportion to its population.

When each caste and subcaste gets its share in proportion to its population, where is the objection to call ourselves Hindu?

The Sikhs in Punjab offer a good example to prove my point. The Sikhs have beautifully and effectively strengthened their **identity**. They have their own party, own state, own religion. Own temple, own **identity**. That is why they don't mind when they are called Hindu by the Brahmins.

When we say Sikhs, we are referring to the upper caste Sikhs who are almost *hinduised*. We are not referring to the Dalit Sikhs. The upper caste Sikhs fought against the Hindus and their struggle for self-determination ultimately climaxed in the "Blue Star Operation". The Hindus got a taste of the ferocity of the Sikhs. Since then the Sikh-Hindu antagonism has very much come down because the Sikhs themselves got *hinduised*. They do not mind calling themselves Hindu or a branch of Hinduism because the Sikh **identity** has brought them power and a bargaining strength. They have become prosperous. They have everything what they want. When a caste or a group of people (**identity**) achieves justice and equality and comes on par with its oppressor, there will be no antagonism between the two. This is what happened with the Sikhs whose main political party is a part of the coalition with the Hindu nazi brahminical party ruling India. ■

✳ ✳ ✳

CHAPTER - XII

Religious conversion

Those interested in fighting and destroying Brahminism will have to give the top-most priority to religious conversion. The Hindu nazi leaders have themselves acknowledged that their religion (Brahminism) would be reduced to a minority by the end of this century. (DV May 16, 2003 p.11: "*Hindus will be a minority by 21st century end?*"). Budhism practically wiped out Brahminism until Adi Shankara came on the scene and launched his violent revivalist activities. No other weapon is as deadly to Brahminism as conversion and that is why promoters of Brahminism are trying to introduce a Central legislation to ban conversions. Some states have their local legislations. Tamil Nadu under a Brahmin Chief Minister recently introduced a ban on conversions. (Dr. B.R. Ambedkar: *Why Go for Conversion?*, DSA-1987).

Dr. Babasaheb Ambedkar experimented with different remedies to liberate the Untouchables and finally arrived at religious conversion to Budhism.

Only road to self-respect

Conversion may not improve the economic status of the converts but it must be noted that poverty is never the problem of the Untouchables. Nowhere our people have complained of poverty. Their problem is denial of human rights, dignity, self-respect. Deprivation. And conversion instantly restores all these. Conversion, therefore, has become the first step in the long march of Dalits towards liberation.

So, no fight against Brahminism will succeed without assigning the top-most priority to conversion.

Convert to which religion? This question will naturally arise. Dr. Babasaheb Ambedkar embraced Budhism. But Tamil Nadu Untouchables preferred Islam. In Kerala and Andhra Pradesh, they went over to Christianity. In Maharashtra, the trend is in favour of Budhism. In Punjab, many Untouchables sought salvation in Sikhism. So in different parts, Dalits preferred different liberating religions according to their convenience. But all over India Untouchables are unanimous on one point that religious conversion is the only road to self-respect.

Some people may ask: when you say that Untouchables are not Hindu, where does the question come of quitting "Hinduism"? Babasaheb has effectively answered this question.

Not born but made Hindu

It is a historical fact that Untouchables are not Hindu. They are human beings. As the original inhabitants of India, they can't be Hindu. Untouchables are not Hindu and were never Hindu. "Hinduism" or Brahminism was an Aryan (foreign) import. The very fact that the upper castes do not allow Untouchables inside their temples proves that our people are not Hindu. In Puri Jagannath Temple, Rajasthan's Nathadwara temple and hundreds of other temples there are boards displayed outside announcing that "entry only for born Hindus". Since Untouchables are not "born Hindu", they are barred. This clearly proves that our people are not "born Hindu".

Three reasons that "make" Dalits Hindu

They are not "born Hindu" but "made Hindu" or called Hindu — that too in the past about 100 years or so. Upper castes resorted to *hinduisation* of Untouchables for three principal reasons:-

1. "Hinduism" becomes the "majority religion" of India only if

Untouchables and Tribals are included in it. Upper castes are fond of bragging that "Hindus" are the India's single largest population. If the Untouchables go out, this "majority" becomes an instant a minority. M.K. Gandhi's life-long effort was to annex these people to "Hinduism" so that it becomes a "majority religion". *Swaraj* or freedom was not his topmost priority.

Untouchables and Tribals put together become a staggering 30% of the Indian population. Even Backward Castes (35%) are neither *shudras* nor Hindus. So if this 30% plus 35%, a total of 65% walk out, Hindus become not only a minority but less than the population of Muslims (15%). That is why this frantic effort to *hinduise* the non-Hindus. And Gandhi was the leader of this movement to *hinduise* us and thus enslave us. But our people are refusing to be fooled.

2. Since every "national" political party including marxist parties are Hindu parties in India, their very existence will be threatened if the *Harijan* vote bank collapses. India's make-believe democracy itself will collapse if the Untouchables walk out of the reigning religion.

State used to promote Hinduism

3. More than anything the very economy of the country, surviving on the slave labour of Untouchables as agricultural labourers, will collapse once the Untouchables embrace other religions and consequently refuse to be slaves and also start migrating to cities.

For these three principal reasons Untouchables who are not "born Hindu" are forcibly "made Hindu" — not in the interest of Untouchables but in the interest of their oppressors. The state itself is used in India to promote Hinduism (DV, Edit. Sept.1, 1987: "*The state used to promote Hindu religion?*"). This becomes very well evident when all of a sudden our "saviours" wake up and start screaming whenever conversions take place. But the same "saviours" are indifferent to Untouchables when our people are kicked, killed, burnt, raped and their little property destroyed by the very upper caste Hindus. That means our "saviours" are not interested in us but interested only in keeping us under "Hinduism" in their interest.

What the enemy loves we must hate and what the enemy hates we must love. This is the Law of Contradictions. Did we not say this?

Some claiming to be our well-wishers ask: "What is the use of conversion? Other religions also have castes. Will it not be a jump from the frying pan to fire?"

Role of conversion

Our reply is:

(1) Yes. We know this better than our "well-wishers". If there is caste in other non-Hindu religions in India, the contagion of caste has gone only from Hinduism. So other religions can't be blamed. In no other religion, caste has religious sanction except Hinduism.

(2) Dr. Babasaheb Ambedkar has given this call for conversion only to our people, Untouchables and those slaves slogging under Hinduism. Not to our oppressors or those slaves enjoying their slavery. So, our "well-wishers" need not bother. We do what is best for our salvation. We are the architect of ourselves.

The social and religious aspirations of Dalits is not only to liberate themselves but through that to save India also. According to Dr. Babasaheb Ambedkar, the Father of India, who conducted a series of experiments in this field, this is possible only through religious conversion. Religious conversion is the best, the simplest, the most inexpensive and also the most nonviolent way of not only liberating the Dalits (which in other words means fighting Brahminism) but also the country as a whole. It is as simple as that.

The upper castes (Hindus) give equal treatment to Christians, Muslims and Sikhs. People belonging to these three sections (called religious minorities) did not come from outside India. Christians of India did not come from Rome. Muslims did not come from Arabia. They are converts from today's SC/ST/BCs. They achieved equality and self-respect only through conversion. When 20% of India (Muslim, Christian and Sikh) could achieve equality and self-respect through such a simple social engineering (conversion), why not the rest of the SC/ST/BCs follow this simple path? When a majority of Dalits convert to other religions, Brahminism is dead.

Never ending caste war

Such a conversion will bring happiness to both SC/ST/BCs as well as their oppressors (Hindus). As long as Dalits remain within the Hindu fold, they have to fight with Hindus daily. It is a daily fight in the countryside today. India is full of caste wars between the Hindus and Dalits. Conversion will once for all end this war and violence and there will be peace in the countryside and India as a whole.

The Hindus may ask: When there is caste inside Muslim, Christian and Sikhs, why again go into such a leaking house? This is our answer: There is a great deal of difference between the Hindu caste system and the caste within other religions. Caste is not the chief characteristic of these religions. But the Hindu caste system has the religious sanction. That is why no Dalit has been made a Shankarachari to this day. But several

Dalits have become Bishops, Imams and Sikh Sants. They can destroy their castes without destroying their religions. But if you destroy caste system Brahminism itself is dead. This is because the caste system is the other name for Hinduism. Kill caste, Hinduism is dead.

Ambedkarites have to be democratic and take into consideration the local needs of the people around and its historical background. In the North Eastern states of India the Mongoloid Tribals preferred Christianity, in Punjab the Dalits went over to Sikhism. In Maharashtra the Dalits followed Dr. Ambedkar to Budhism. As Ambedkarites we cannot compel those seeking freedom from Brahminical oppression to prefer only Budhism. No doubt it was Dr. Ambedkar's choice. But the Untouchables, did not wholesale follow their father and Saviour. Religious freedom will have to be given to those seeking conversion and depending upon the pull and push of a particular liberating religion in a particular region. The people will accept the best religion of their choice.

Brahminism will meet with sure death whatever may be the religion to which you convert. ∎

CHAPTER - XIII

Task before map-makers of India

It took nearly 60 years for India's hungry masses to understand why they are hungry. Even now, we don't think they have understood the situation and identified the enemy. Every political party is controlled by the upper caste exploiters and the Brahmin-dominated media is diverting the attention of hungry masses from their exploitation to non-issues.

Brahminical strategies and tactics may be so superior and flawless to keep the masses hungry and enslaved. And yet it may not be possible for a mere 3% of the *vaidiks* to control such a mass of humanity in this country of over 1,000 millions. That is how this micro-minority of *vaidiks* is also getting nervous and realising its physical and numerical weaknesses.

Hindutva graduates into Moditva

This is evident from the growth of violent Hindu nazism. The Gujarat Genocide-2002 is, therefore, an important development because all the Hindu false propaganda that the Hindu stands for non-violence has fallen flat. The ruling upper castes (Hindu) have started showing their nervousness. For the first time they have started using the state machinery itself to commit violence on the masses. This is an important and welcome development.

In this chapter, I am outlining a new thesis to deal with the fast developing situations to convert a problem into an opportunity. I call it the task before the map-makers of the 21st century India. In other words, the shape of the things to come when nation-states rock the sub-continent.

How will the map of India look in the next millennium? What will be the shape and size of the sub-continent which the map-makers of India will have to draw? How will the *Moditva* (the graduated form of *Hindutva* or Hindu nazism, deriving its name from Narendra Modi who caused the Gujarat Genocide - 2002) managers drive their uncontrollable Hindu nazi bulldozer trampling the starving millions?

India has had turbulent times. Ever since it became "independent" (1947), it had no peace. It was one civil war after the other. The country has been passing from crisis to more crisis — ever-lasting crisis. A tiny 15% of micro-minority Brahminical Social Order (Aryans) took over the leadership, headed by the most crooked, cunning and crafty *vaidiks*, which jumped into the 21st century pushing the rest of the 85% of the oppressed Bahujans back to poverty, illiteracy, disease, unemployment, beggary, prostitution. A permanent slavery.

Dr. Ambedkar Era

With the active connivance of the ever-willing "national" toilet papers, the rulers have hammered into our heads that India is a "nation" and its 1,000 million population is "one people" and the religion of the overwhelming majority is Hinduism. Rewriting of history became a "national" industry almost developing it into a fine art of denial of history. Murli Manohar Joshi, the crafty Allahabad *vaidik*, is presenting before us a new history, new geography and a new sociology based on his *jati* guru Chanakya's pattern.

Will the map-makers of the 21st century India (DV called it "Dr. Ambedkar Era") follow this false, fabricated *vaidik* version? What will India look like as the cursed *Gandhi yug* (20th century) comes to a close and "Dr. Ambedkar Era" begins?

We examine this question so that the non-Aryan indigenous people of India may properly guide their children to step into the "Dr. Ambedkar Era". Very careful preparation will have to begin and if necessary we can hold a strategy session on how to prepare ourselves to welcome the long-awaited "Dr. Ambedkar Era."

Every ism in India has failed. I had made this clear in my Nagpur speech (DV Aug.1, 1999 p.13: *"Brahminism swallowing Ambedkarite Movement also?"*). The list of failed isms (marxism, gandhism, naxalism, JP's Total Revolution, now the latest Hindu nazism) is too long. Only the time-tested Ambedkarism remains, the only lighthouse in this dark subcontinent submerged under the weight of the Brahminical Social Order (BSO).

Why we like Narendra Modi

The BSO might have mesmerised us through its mass media to call India a "nation" and maintained some artificial "unity" with the help of its mighty physical force through its police and armed forces. It might have also over-awed us by the *Moditva* wave that tricked Ahmedabad Dalits to kill Muslims in thousands in the year 2002 and then win the Gujarat elections.

Nothing of it need perturb us. All this is for our good. It is these Hindu nazis who provoked the Muslims and Christians who for the first time started openly attacking Brahminism. Thanks to *Moditva*, Brahminism for the first time came on the lips of Muslims and Christians. Thanks to *Moditva*, Muslims and Christians have started thinking of Dalits and joining hands with us. Two sleeping slaves of India, Muslims and Christians, have at last woken up. Should we not thank Narendra Modi?

The ruling class (BSO) itself is not united. One Aryan fellow is cutting another Aryan's throat. Caste, language and geographical diversity is tearing apart every society, every province, every people. The pulls and pressures are extremely sharp and things have started reaching the breaking point. Is this not a welcome development? Should we not thank the Hindu nazis for bringing caste, India's most ancient and the only mark of identifying a social group, to the election arena in a big way?

Neither the ruling BSO (15%) is a homogenous whole nor the ruled Bahujans (85%) are one single united house.

India is not a nation and was never a nation. It is a country of several nations, said Dr. Babasaheb Ambedkar, Father of India (DV Sept.1, 1991: "*India is not yet a nation: Dr. Ambedkar's historic speech in the Constituent Assembly on Nov.4, 1948*"). This is coming true as India enters the 21st century. What will be the task of the map-maker's of India of the "Dr. Ambedkar Era?"

Self-determination

The bitter experience of the past 56 years has finally taught the Bahujans (the SC/ST/BCs and the Muslims/Christians/ Sikhs) that if India has to remain peaceful and contented each and every "nation" within India has to exercise its right of self-determination by which alone it can regain its lost human rights.

The Vajpayees, the Narendra Modis, the Murli Manohar Joshis alone cannot rule India and the rest remain as their slaves. Every "nation" has now realised the importance of equal sharing and equal caring. You cannot put your hand into my pocket and steal while I go on working.

It is not the non-Aryan Dravidian races comprising the Bahujans alone that lost their human rights. Even the *shudras* forming 90% of the BSO (Hindu) are also complaining that they are only used as the fighting arm of the *vaidiks* who are not even 5%.

The Kshatriyas and Vaishyas also feel neglected. The BSO comprising 15% of the population "unites" only to oppress the non-Aryan Bahujans. During the rest of the period they are permanently on war with each other. Even the father of their own nation, M.K. Gandhi (a Vaishya), was shot dead by a Brahmin as part of this war.

Vivekananda, Chinmayananda, Jayaprakash Narayan, Lal Bahadur Shastri, H.D. Deve Gowda, Bal Thackeray, all noted *shudra* leaders, were ridiculed and routed. Even V.P. Singh, a Kshatriya, was not tolerated as Prime Minister. L.K. Advani, Home Minister – the man who made BJP (*Brahmana Jati Party*) a ruling party — is never given his due place.

This stupid Narendra Modi, a Backward Caste fellow, will be fully used by the *vaidiks* and dumped into dust bin. What happened to Kalyan Singh, Bangaru Laxman, Vaghela, Ram Vilas Paswan? The *vaidiks* are experts in using the idiots and then discarding them.

Caste contradictions

Caste contradictions are killing the Hindus. Dr. Babasaheb Ambedkar wrote a book itself (*Annihilation of Caste*) to save Hindus from their caste system. When these handful of Hindus themselves are so much a house divided how can India become a Hindu nation? The thinking section among Hindus itself is deeply worried over the chaos setting in although it is hiding the cracks and fissures of the periodical hypnotic stunts managed through the mass media it controls.

What then will be the task of the map-makers of India of the "Dr. Ambedkar Era?" Cartographers have a big job to redraw the map of India. Will the Aryan rulers be able to avert this impending cartographical catastrophe? That brings us to the star question. What is that question? The question is: *Hindutva* now modified into *Moditva* is hastening the break up of India on caste lines. Is this not a contradiction? No. The nazis are doing all this to "unite" India and make it a *Hindu Rashtra*. And in doing that they are actually breaking up India on caste, religious and linguistic lines. Should we not thank them? Did we not say: "Strengthen every *jati* (nation), Hinduism will be dead?" (DV Editorial Dec.16, 1993). That is why we have been saying that "Sacred Brahmins" are any day better than "Socialist Brahmins".

Meaning of "Sacred" & "Socialist Brahmins"

By "Sacred Brahmins" we mean all those Hindu nazis who aggressively and violently enforce their Hindu nazi rule calling Muslims as terrorists, anti-nationals, cow-killers, Pakistani agents and do everything to *hinduise* Muslims and Christians. If they do not surrender, the "Sacred Brahmins" do not mind killing them. Babri Masjid demolition, hundreds of anti-Muslim riots, the Kashmir war and violence, Gujarat Genocide are all the work of these "Sacred Brahmins" who want to enforce the decisions of the founding fathers of the Hindu nazi party, RSS like V.D. Savarkar, B.G. Tilak, Golwalkar etc. The "Sacred Brahmins" are honest because they mean what they say and say what they mean. The Muslims, Christians, Dalits and all other persecuted nationalities have no confusion about them and find no difficulty in identifying them. The "Sacred Brahmins" are our honest enemies.

As against this the "Sacred Brahmins", there is another section of *vaidiks* who parade as great friends of the Muslims, Christians, Dalits, Tribals but actually give them slow poison. They kill our people by deceiving our people. This class of "Socialist Brahmins" are more dangerous because the enemy is not even honest in its hatred of our people who being poor, illiterate and gullible will mistake them to be friends, trust them and ultimately get deceived. The marxists, gandhians belong to this category. Between the two sections of Brahmins, we prefer the "Sacred Brahmins". We have written a book itself, *Dialogue of the Bhoodevatas* (DSA -1993) in which we have given the true character of the two varieties of Brahmins. The true face of the "Sacred Brahmins" is now visible.

Look how beautifully the *Moditva* has modified the *Hindutva*. M.K. Gandhi asked the Muslims, Dalits and every other slaves to sleep. *Moditva* whipped up these sleeping slaves. And today every section is agitated. Angry. Is this not a welcome development?

Thoughts on Pakistan

That is why we want the Hindu nazis to get one more term in Delhi so that they will complete the job of dividing India so that the job of the map-makers of the "Dr. Ambedkar Era" will become easy to complete the new map of India.

When Dr. Babasaheb Ambedkar has categorically said India is not a nation but a country of several nations, what actually did he mean? What then is "nation?"

Babasaheb has very beautifully answered this question in his book, *Thoughts on Pakistan — Pakistan or Partition?* (W&S, Vol.8, Govt. of Maharashtra, 1990). It is already proved that Hindus are not a nation. Muslims too are not a nation. But Muslims constitute India's single largest "community". Sikhs too have proved that they are not a nation. Scheduled Castes (Dalits) who form the single largest population of India (20%) are a collection of several castes and subcastes. Tribals are divided into scores of ethnic identities. ∎

* * *

CHAPTER - XIV

In defence of "Sacred Brahmins"

Remember our oft-repeated warning. This micro-minority of about 3% Aryan Brahminical forces had never failed even once in their attempt to defeat and enslave the non-Aryan natives ever since they divided, defeated, destroyed and finally drove Budhism out of India. By the end of the 10th century, Budhism was practically stamped out of India.

To them it was success after success. Such was their dedication, devotion and concentration on their mission to establish the "Brahman Raj" which today they are selling as *Hindutva* or Hindu nationalism. The name goes on changing. But the content remains the same. The name may not be "Hinduism" in another 50 years. Please read the book, *History of Hindu Imperialism* (1941) written by an upper caste Malayali (Nair) monk, Swami Dharma Thirtha. (Blumoon Books, New Delhi). He says:

> "Brahminism never stood for any religious doctrine or faith, Its life and soul, then, as it is now, was the caste system with the Brahman as the highest sacerdotal caste, and its vital interest was priestly exploitation". (p. 108).

Vaidiks & Hinduism

The alien Brahminical forces have no permanent ideology, no permanent god or no permanent religion. The only thing permanent with them is their interests in their properties, position and power.

The Brahminical forces never had any interest in Hinduism or *Hindutva* or even their gods. Their sole interest has been caste system (the other name for Hinduism) which enables the *Vaidik* Brahmins to lord over this land. The *vaidiks* have manufactured several "scriptures", epics and "philosophies" with different names. All of them, including gandhism, marxism, socialism, Hinduism are all means to the same end — that is casteism.

Ever since the death of Budhism it was a smooth ride for Brahminism. Neither the Muslim rule nor the British (Christian) rule came in their way of *hinduising* (enslaving) the indigenous Bahujans. Its most noteworthy achievement was in renaming and then amalgamating the hundreds of tribes among the Bahujans into their castes (*jati*) and then grading them hierarchically into their caste system (*Varnashrama Dharma*) and finally placing the Brahmin at the apex of this caste pyramid. The caste system finally ensured the supremacy of the *vaidik*. We have said all this in our book *Brahminism* (DSA-2002).

Tributes to *vaidik* miracles

I don't want to go into the details of all these *vaidik* tricks to ensure their supremacy. What I can say is the *vaidiks* have accomplished a miracle unknown in world history. Springing up from the ashes, to which Budhism once reduced them, they were mysteriously reborn. Then they regrouped and retaliated with a vengeance. Hats off to Brahmin patience, perseverance and the love for their *jati*. All these have been discussed many times in DV and our books.

My point is that the *vaidiks* have been achieving success after success because anything they touch turns into mud. Never did they face defeat.

The advent of M.K. Gandhi and his transformation as Mahatma was a carefully crafted Brahminical strategy. The mask of the "Socialist Brahmin" that he was made to wear was meant to deceive primarily the Dalits and Muslims. The Gujarati Bania gets the credit for partitioning India "to get rid of the Muslims" and handing over the truncated India to the *vaidiks* by making a Kashmiri Brahmin, Jawaharlal Nehru, as the first Prime Minister of India.

Dr. Ambedkar fought Gandhi

Gandhi deceived the Dalits ("Poona Pact"), Tribals, the Muslims, Sikhs and Christians and preached "non-violence" to the hungry stomachs but at the same time encouraged upper caste violence. The credit for ushering in the *vaidik* rule in "independent" India goes solely to Gandhi and not to today's Hindu Nazi Bharatiya Janata Party (BJP). It was Gandhi who tried to *hinduise* (enslave) the Dalits, Tribals and Backward Castes and made them slaves of Brahmins. The only person who fought Gandhi in pre-independent India was Dr. Babasaheb Ambedkar after Jinnah left for Pakistan.

Gandhi's Congress Party ruled the country for 50-long years and ensured the further enslavement of the Dalits, Muslims etc. and at the same time further strengthened the muscles of the overfed upper castes. The Congress Party has no right to criticise the Hindu nazis of today because Gandhi's Congress itself was then India's original brahminical party, as Babasaheb had said.

Honest Brahmins

As long as the Congress ruled India, the deprived Bahujans remained doped and mesmerised. The Dalits and Muslims, the two most virile and yet the worst persecuted sections, were almost totally with the Congress. Like those innocent cows licking the very hand of the butcher leading them to slaughter-house, these two communities were continuously voting for the Congress and getting slaughtered.

The rise of the BJP changed the country's social scene. This Hindu nazi party completely guided by its Hindu nazi secret organisation, RSS, is made out of a different metal. It is a party of "Sacred Brahmins" who are more honest in their words and deeds. They are not deceptive and double-tongued like Gandhi and his Congress, the party of "Socialist Brahmins".

Between the "Sacred Brahmins" and the "Socialist Brahmins" we have always said that we liked the first one, the "Sacred Brahmins". This is the thesis of our book, *Dialogue of the Bhoodevatas*. Because they are honest, straight-forward. They mean what they say and say what they mean. Hence we can trust them. "Socialist Brahmins" like Gandhi, Nehru, JP etc. will smile and smile and yet cut your throat painlessly without you being aware of it. But the "Sacred Brahmins" openly hate you and publicly abuse you.

We like fire-makers

"Sacred Brahmins" are fire-makers. They burn, loot and murder. But the "Socialist Brahmins" are fire-fighters. They extinguish the fire. They pour cold water on our burning anger. They say they love Dalits but give you slow poison. Slaves of India enjoying their slavery for thousands of years need somebody who will push them into a crisis and force them to get up and fight. "Sacred Brahmins" whip up the slaves, make them angry and then make them fight and die for their liberation. Who is better?

Gujarat election

"Socialist Brahmins" will push the chances of Indian revolution backwards, dope you with their deadly *karma* theory, lull you into sleep with their sweet lullabies. But the "Sacred Brahmins" will make you get up and fight. They will sharpen the contradictions and hence help hasten the Indian revolution. Hence this thesis: *In defence of Sacred Brahmins.*

We are happy the Hindu nazis have routed the "Socialist Brahmin" party of Congress in the 2002 Gujarat Assembly election and even ridiculed Vaidik Vajpayee and relegated him to the background. We welcome this development which unveils the real face of Hinduism.

Never believe a word of what Vajpayee says. The "Socialist Brahmins" of India are keeping Vajpayee at the top to deceive the Dalits, Muslims, BCs and other persecuted nationalities of India.

Vajpayee is today what M.K. Gandhi was yesterday. The ruling upper castes yesterday wanted an expert who could deceive the angry, starving masses and lull them to sleep. They discovered an ideal person in Gandhi. But as soon as Gandhi handed over the country to the *vaidiks*, an honest "Sacred Brahmin" from Pune came to Delhi, purchased a revolver and shot dead the bogus Mahatma. Gandhi's work was over. *Vaidiks* no longer needed his services. (V.T. Rajshekar, *Why Godse Killed Gandhi?*, DSA-1997).

Modi proves Vajpayee wrong

Vajpayee like Gandhi is the false face of *Hindutva* to deceive the Dalits, Muslims, Tribals and Backward Castes. Narendra Modi of Gujarat came and proved Vajpayee wrong. The "Sacred Brahmins", whom we like for their intellectual honesty, do not agree with Vajpayee's interpretation of Hinduism just as the "Sacred Brahmins" then represented by Tilak, Godse, Savarkar, Golwalkar etc. did not agree with Gandhi.

Please note that India's *vaidik* vampire has not changed even a bit since centuries. They do not believe in change. Because their religion is called *Sanatana Dharma* which is a never-changing political weapon intended to keep the *vaidiks* as rulers.

To repeat: Between the "Sacred" and "Socialist Brahmins", we like the former. It is their violent attacks on Muslims and Christians that finally made the two communities angry and

revolt against Hinduism. Until then, both were believing the
humbug of secularism which the Congress was selling

religion. Secularists and "Socialist Brahmins" are hiding this to deceive our people.

Vajpayee's bluffs

No less a person than B.G. Tilak, one of the founding fathers of the Hindu nazi party, said Hinduism fully sanctioned violence. *Manu Dharma Sastra* sanctioned immediate killing. (D.K. Gosavi: *Tilak, Gandhi & Gita*, Bharatiya Vidya Bhawan, Bombay - 1983).

Vajpayee is using some "Socialist Brahmin" slogans to confuse and then deceive the Dalits, Tribals and BCs who might otherwise revolt against his nazi party just as the Muslims and Christians did when they came to know the truth.

Failure to identify enemy

Vajpayee played a trick in his "Goa musings" with secularism — a much abused word in Hindu India. But his "Sacred Brahmin" comrade, Ashok Singhal, quickly hit back when he said VHP's next target was secularism — a cover for the "Socialist Brahmins" to fool the Bahujans. "Sacred Brahmins" don't believe in secularism. Many humbugs and frauds flourished in India by trading on secularism. The fake human rights movement in India is packed with "secular" Brahmins. The environmental movement, animal-lovers, tree-lovers, women's movement, NGOs are all dangerous secularists. We have to thank the "Sacred Brahmins" for tearing this mask of secularists. We congratulate Singhal for his honest observations.

The greatest defect of "Socialist Brahmins" is they give a

"enemies of Hindus" and "anti-nationals". In other words, the "enemy of the Hindu" is identified and once the enemy is identified it is easy to target the enemy, attack and finish the enemy. The Gujarat Genocide-2002 was the result of identifying the enemy.

The Evil must be called by its name

There is no point in giving an hour-long lecture on your enemy without identifying the enemy. The Evil must be called by its name. It is only after the "Sacred Brahmins" started identifying the Muslims and Christians and started violently attacking them, the two communities have started getting angry and mobilised themselves against the Hindu nazis.

But the moment the Muslim, Christians and even Dalits start getting angry, the "Socialist Brahmins" with the help of their Brahmin-dominated "national" media quickly jump into action and start misleading the angry masses. The "Socialist Brahmin" criticisms are always vague. They say the "communal violence" is created by the "Hindu right", a term which means nothing. If there is a "Hindu right", which is the "Hindu left"? The "Socialist Brahmins" do not want to identify the *vaidiks* behind the violence against Muslims, Christians etc. That is why they use such vague, meaningless words. This is the mischief of the "Socialist Brahmins" and because of this mischief the villain remains unidentified, hidden and the angry Muslim, Christian and Dalits get misguided. Identify the Enemy. The Evil must be called by its name.

That is why we say the "Sacred Brahmins" are much better. They are our honest enemies. But our real enemy is the "Socialist Brahmins" who are more dangerous and a menace that must be finished first.

The "secularists" are more dangerous than the "communalists".

The "secularists" are worried that if they identify the "communalists", the historical Brahmin hegemony over the Dalit-Backward Castes would be lost. These upper caste "secularists" want to shield "Hindu communalism" because the perpetrators of the crime are their own cousins. If they identify the criminals, the Muslims and Dalits, the victims, would target their *jatwalas*, and the Brahmin leadership would be lost. The upper caste "liberals" therefore are more dangerous than the "communal" Brahmins.

Remember one thing. When the "Socialist Brahmin" Vajpayee speaks some sweet sounding words, it is the RSS which makes him say all this to keep the SC/ST/BCs in good humour. The nazis cannot afford to antagonise the whole lot of the obedient, unpaid, permanent, and loyal slaves of Hindus. The Hindu nazism can only devour and digest SC/ST/BCs one by one. Not all at once.

Dalits made to hate Muslims

The *vaidiks* have succeeded in *hinduising* (enslaving) the SC/ST/BCs to a great extent and thereby making them hate the Muslims. That job has been fairly well done. In Ahmedabad, it was the Dalits who attacked and killed the Muslims and caused the Gujarat Genocide-2002. It was the Dalits who climbed up the Babri Masjid and destroyed its dome. In Delhi, it was the Tribals and BCs who killed thousands of Sikhs when Indira Gandhi was killed.

The Muslims are still a big force forming 15% of the population. They are a revolutionary community. They have international support also. Besides, a powerful Pakistan, a nuclear power, is beside India. So, the Hindu nazis can stage only a single Gujarat Genocide-2002 but if they repeat it elsewhere, there will be a turmoil and wholesale bloodbath forcing even the

SC/ST/BCs to turn against the nazis. This fear is real and genuine.

Hinduising Muslims

The nazis want mainly Dalits to remain with them until they completely "finish" the Muslims. "Finishing" does not mean killing Muslims wholesale. This is neither possible nor practicable. Such a big number of Muslims cannot be killed. What they will do is try the "Spanish Experiment" of *hinduising* the Muslims. The elite Muslims, who often sing the Hindu-Muslim unity song, have been already *hinduised* (enslaved) to a great extent. Once the Muslims are "finished", the next target is Dalits.

How to make Dalits angry

In fact, the *vaidiks* hate Dalits much more than the Muslims. The job of "finishing" the Dalits will be expedited when the "Sacred Brahmins" come to power on their own strength without the support of any allies. Then only Dalits, like today's Muslims, will get angry.

The "Socialist Brahmins" like the Congress, the Marxists, Vajpayee etc. will deceive the Dalits, mislead them and lull them to sleep. And then quietly suck their blood in painless operation. But "Sacred Brahmins" resort to open attack, murder and mayhem as they did in Gujarat Genocide-2002 which totally turned Muslims against the nazi party.

If the Dalits have to turn against the nazis and their Hinduism, the "Sacred Brahmins" of the *Moditva* brand must come to power in Delhi. Then only the Dalits will be whipped up from their deep slumber and made to get angry. We want the Dalits to get angry. And the one sure people who are capable of making them angry are the "Sacred Brahmins". Not the "Socialist Brahmins". That is why we like the "Sacred

Brahmins". Knowing this full well, the nazis are going step by step to keep the SC/ST/BCs under their wings. They are not in a hurry. That is why Vajpayee is now and then called upon by the RSS to utter some falsehood to mislead the Dalits and keep them confused.

Adi Shankara founded RSS

In this mock fight between the "Socialist Brahmins" within the Hindu nazi party led by Vajpayee and the "Sacred Brahmins" led by L.K. Advani, Narendra Modi, Togadia, Giriraj Kishore etc., I prefer the latter. I like the honest words of Giriraj dubbing Vajpayee as pseudo-Hindu meaning anti-Hindu. The Vishwa Hindu Parishad (VHP) criticised Vajpayee's "Goa musings" asserting that "no Hindu can be narrow, rigid and extremist". (*Hindu*, Jan.1, 2003).

Hinduism, as represented by the Kerala dwarf Namboodiri Brahmin, Adi Shankara, is "narrow, rigid and extremist". This is Hinduism. Adi Shankara was the real founder of RSS. The Hindu has to be violent. Then only he can be a good Hindu. Even the Hindu god Krishna advocated killing in his *Bhagawad Gita*.

Tilak's interpretation of Hinduism

Bal Gangadhar Tilak (1856-1920) is India's highest authority on the "sacred scriptures" of Brahmins. His interpretation of the *Gita* practically follows that of the Adi Shankara (788-820 AD). Tilak's *Gita Rahasya* (1936, First Edition, Tilak Brother, 568-Narayan Peth, Poona - 411 030) is the best book on the *Bhagawat Gita*. Manu, the Brahmin law-giver, sanctions the immediate killing (Manu VIII-35). The *Mahabharata* suggests circumstances in which falsehood is preferred to truth. When good means prove ineffective one should use the other effective means also to resist evil (meaning anything against the interest of *vaidiks*), he says. This is the interpretation given by the honest "Sacred Brahmin" Tilak. He differs from the whole class of "Socialist Brahmins" like Gandhi. That is why Tilak is hailed as one of the greatest Brahmin leaders and that is how he became one of the founding fathers of the RSS, the most important secret organisation to protect Brahmin interests. We like "Sacred Brahmins" because they speak out the Truth.

Never believe a word of Vajpayee

The "Socialist Brahmins" among *vaidiks* are deeply worried that the "Sacred Brahmin" *Moditva* may rock the boat too much and the boat may sink. That is why they are asking Vajpayee now and then to bluff and mislead the masses so that they will not get angry.

Both the "Socialist" and "Sacred Brahmins" have the same goal — establishment of the "Brahmin Raj". The "Socialist Brahmins" being the more dangerous lot, they are more eager to establish their "Brahmin Raj". But their fear is that in doing so the "Sacred Brahmins" may rock the boat too much. The "Socialist Brahmins" are afraid that the situation may go out of control and the angry masses may identify the hidden enemy who is behind the hate-mongering and the uncontrollable social unrest. That is why they are now and then fielding Vajpayee to mislead and bluff. Never believe a word of what Vajpayee says. He is the Gandhi of the Hindu nazi party.

Martyrdom of Vajpayee

There is even a fear among loyal followers of Vajpayee that the "Sacred Brahmins" may do a Gandhi out of him. Remember, it was an honest "Sacred Brahmin", Nathuram Godse, who killed Gandhi and made him a "martyr". After killing Gandhi the *vaidik* vampire silently rejoiced but publicly shed crocodile tears. They heaved a sigh of relief that they were able to get rid of the Gujarati Bania once he completed his job of handing over India to *vaidiks*. The RSS even today distributes sweets on the day (Jan.30 every year) Gandhi was assassinated.

Dalit and Backward Caste blind followers of Vajpayee fear that there may be a repetition of this episode. The "Sacred Brahmin" charge is that Vajpayee is already a spent force. Physically he is ruined. At the most he may prolong for an year or two. The "Sacred Brahmins" have already taken over the party but still they find it difficult to sell the party to Dalits, BCs and particularly Muslims.

So, from all these angles "Sacred Brahmins" are always better than the "Socialist Brahmins" because they alone are capable of disturbing the stinking, still waters of this cesspool called "Hindu India".

India's great puppet show

Narendra Modi has blood on his hand. But Vajpayee has a mischievous smile on his face. Vajpayee deceives but Modi provokes. Vajpayee smiles and smiles and yet stabs you in the back. But Modi frightens you, angers you, provokes you and forces you to fight. Now, say who is better? The open, honest enemy? Or the crooked, dishonest friend?

Never believe a word of Vajpayee. He is misleading us. The real Hindu is Modi, Togadia, Giriraj and the RSS which is holding all the strings and managing India's great puppet show.

We don't agree with the Congress Party of "Socialist Brahmins" trying to interpret Hinduism. The Congress Working Committee resolution of Jan.5, 2003 said "Hindu *dharma* has nothing to do with narrow, bigoted *Hindutva*" (*Hindu*, Jan.6, 2003). This Gandhi's party of humbugs is packed with plenty of "Socialist Brahmins" and they have to utter such misleading words to deceive Muslims and Dalits. M.K. Gandhi's Congress is hiding the truth to mislead the Dalits and Muslims — its vote bank.

Whipping up sleeping slaves

So, we can't leave it to the Congress to fight the Hindu nazi party. We can't trust the Congress. It is the party of Gandhis and Nehrus who deceived us. It is the party which Babasaheb fought life long. The Hindu nazi party is more honest. It was the Congress under the leadership of Gandhi that inaugurated the "Brahmin Raj" in India headed by Nehru.

This Hindu nazi party can be tackled and defeated only by the Bahujans. None else is better suited for this job than the Dalits, the children of Babasaheb.

But the real battle will begin once the Hindu nazis conclude that they have "finished" with the Muslims. And then start tackling the Dalits.

Muslim surrender

Muslims would have revolted all over India after the Gujarat Genocide-2002 but the elite Muslim leadership maintained a strict control on the masses and prevented any chances of the masses taking to *Jehad*. The Muslims would have joined the Dalit-Muslim unity movement but the Muslim leadership, corrupted and co-opted and fully under the control of Hindus, did not evince any sincere interest in the movement. The Hindu nazis are fully aware of the Muslim leadership weaknesses and encouraged them to commit more and more acts of betrayal against their own poor, innocent Muslim masses.

The very fact that the entire Muslims of India simply kept quiet after the Gujarat Genocide-2002 proved the weakness of the community. The Gujarat Genocide-2002 has given the hint to

Hindu nazis that the Muslims can be now tackled without any problem.

The corrupt elite Muslims

In the Gujarat Genocide-2002 about 2,000 Muslims have been killed in cold blood. And the Muslims simply died without offering any resistance. Not even a murmur. Muslims may be peace-loving but they are an inflammable commodity. How then in Ahmedabad they died like flies and ants?

This is because of the tremendous influence of the "Socialist Brahmins" on the upper class "secular" Muslims. Over 95% of Indian Muslims are kept poor and made daily victims of violence. And yet they are forced to maintain peace because of the tremendous influence the Muslim religious leadership wields on this poor Muslims. This religious leadership, fully corrupted and co-opted, is part of the Muslim elite which is the sole cause of the continued anti-Muslim war and violence. In the name of "Hindu-Muslim unity" and having close relationship with the Congress Party and other "Socialist Brahmins", the elite Muslims have been always keeping the Muslim masses gagged.

Once the Gujarat Genocide-2002 starts repeating as a result of the "Sacred Brahmin" actions of the *Moditva* brand, the Muslim nerve will start cracking and the masses will refuse to obey the dictates of the elite Muslims and then they will start revolting.

It is at this stage the Muslim masses will break away from the upper class-caste elite Muslims, who kept them away from joining hands with the similarly persecuted Dalits, and then forge Dalit-Muslim unity all over India.

"Socialist Brahmins" by corrupting the elite Muslims prevented the Dalit-Muslim unity but the "Sacred Brahmins" by staging more Godhras and Gujarat Genocides will force the Dalit-Muslim unity.

Who is better? "Socialist" or "Sacred Brahmins"?

Not only that. There will be yet another historic development at this stage. The angry Muslim masses having broken away from the grip of its *moulanas* and *mullahs*, and after having identified the elite Muslims as their internal enemy, which refused to come to their aid in all previous Hindu war and violence on them, will then turn against their own elite Muslims.

Internal enemy of Muslims

This internal enemy so far hiding, wearing the mask of Islam, will be finally identified at this stage. The masses will then realise that they will not be able to fight the external Hindu enemy unless they first eliminate the more dangerous internal enemy. The internal enemy is always more dangerous than the external one. Hence the elite Muslims will have to be tackled first before engaging the Hindu nazis.

When the angry Muslim masses turn against its own upper class-caste elite Muslims, there is a chance of the latter falling in line as Islam is a disciplined religion which will make them realise their crime and make quick corrections. The binding force of Islam will unify the whole community and the entire Muslim *ummah* may then stand as one man. Such a chance is not ruled out.

The Muslims today are a house divided. Too much of jealousy and distrust has weakened the once ruling race of India. Should we not thank the "Sacred Brahmins" if they force the elite Muslims to surrender to the angry Muslim masses and then bring about a solid unity of the whole community?

Turning point of history

This will be an interesting turning point in the history of the country after the 1947 partition of India. During this period it was the elite Muslims who fled away to Pakistan leaving their poor, persecuted religious brothers to the Hindu wolves. The rise of the Hindu nazism, violently pushed ahead by the "Sacred Brahmins", will force the poor, jobless Muslims to finally identify the elite Muslims as their real enemy.

The Muslim masses were misled by the Muslim elite which went on impressing upon its poor religious brothers that they were victims of "Hindu communalism". But it was not a Hindu-Muslim war. The upper castes (Hindu) used the non-Hindu Dalits and BCs to attack and kill the poor Muslims in their good old game of divide and rule. The elite Muslims refused to analyse these and place the facts before the poor Muslim masses because the rich Muslims have close connections with Hindus and some of them are Hindu converts.

Flow of foreign funds

The elite Muslims should have identified the Brahminical forces and called upon the community to target the real enemy. They did not do it. They failed in their duty. This is the greatest crime committed by the elite Muslims against their own poor Muslim brethren. The elite Muslims send their children to convents, live in Hindu areas, have their account in Hindu banks, have Hindu lawyers and chartered accountants. Their entire control is in the hands of Hindus. In fact these elite Muslims getting foreign funds through the Foreign Contributions Regulation Act (FCRA) share their loot with the Hindus since the Home Ministry which controls the FCRA is Hindu-dominated. All the rich Muslims are fully under the Hindu control. Many times it is the Hindus who direct the elite Muslims on how it has to speak, act and behave with the Muslim masses and Dalits.

Dalit-Muslim unity

Once the Gujarat Genocide-2002 starts repeating, the entire Muslim masses will get heated up, get unfastened and liberated from the clutches of its elite Muslim control.

This will be an interesting and welcome development in the history of India —very conducive for a revolutionary upsurge in the struggle of the oppressed. This will lead to a double development:- (1) the Muslim masses will finally identify their enemy within the community and (2) also their real, genuine allies — Dalits — in their common struggle. There will be a spontaneous movement for Dalit-Muslim unity at this stage and a simultaneous outburst against the elite Muslims who have been keeping the lid tight on the boiling anger of the Muslim masses.

Islam minus god

The Muslim elite may opt to remain ignorant of history and the trends of history. But the Muslims were the first to opt for the egalitarianism of marxism in the twenties. The founding father of India's Communist Party was not the Brahmin S.A. Dange, but Moulana Hasrat Mohani, who had declared "communism as Islam minus god, and with god added, it is nothing but Islam". The Bathists of Iraq and Syria had done the same. So also the Muslims of the underbelly of Russia, now independent nations. This was in the twenties. While this Islamic socialism clicked among the Arabs and others it was suppressed in India by the "Socialist Brahmins" under Gandhi and the Congress leading to anti-Muslimism and partition of India. Had not this happened, India would have gone under Islamic socialism led by Muslims followed by Dalits and

Backward Castes. This revolution was lost — thanks to a Brahmin conspiracy under Gandhi.

Communist Muslims

Hasrat Mohani was not alone. So great an Islamist like Dr. Iqbal was also a votary of communism plus god. He was followed by a host of great Muslims like Josh Malihabadi, Kwaja Ahmed Abbas, producer-director Mahboob Khan (through films), Sahir Ludhianavi, Sajjad Zahir. The greatest Urdu poet of our days, Z. Ansari, is yet a communist.

Even at the mass level, the Muslims of Bengal fought for economic egalitarianism along with god through communism. Their political party was not the Muslim League upto 1937. It was Krishik Praja Party (agriculturist peoples party). Even to this day they are communists in West Bengal. So also a good chunk of Muslims in Kerala are communists.

Apart from economic egalitarianism, Muslims had a programme to destroy Western imperialism (British empire in India) with the political might of communism. While this programme failed in India, it succeeded in Iraq, Syria and the Turkic states of the under belly of Russia (Uzbekistan etc.). The Turkic states are now free and the Bathists of Iraq and Syria are still struggling. Communism was taken as an international strategy to fight for the liberation of Muslims who were the poorest all over the world in the twenties.

Attack on Muslim elites

After 1947, the "Socialist Brahmins" realised this potential and started using communism to promote the cause of Brahminism but the "Sacred Brahmins" will push the Muslims into communist methodology if not the communist ideology and the first victims will be the Muslim elites.

Earlier, Muslimism had made the Muslim masses the protectors of Muslim elites who had some concern for the poor Muslims. Now that the Muslim elites have broken this bondage of Muslimism, poor Muslims will give up their concern and attack the Muslim elites who are the nearest to them.

Thus, the Muslim elites will be the first victims of the ensuing revolution. And once the Muslim masses start attacking the Muslim elites, Dalits will become "Hindu" and start attacking Hindu elites. But as the Dalit elites are not rich they will be spared. Dalits will then join the Muslims. India will then get divided into haves and have-nots.

Punjab blood bath

The "Sacred Brahmins" have already sown the seeds for this Dalit-Muslim unity of have-nots by giving them both the common bondage of poverty and unemployment and the consequent leisure to think and the time to act. The job opportunities of Dalits are destroyed through privatisation and computerisation. Muslims similarly kept unemployed had gone for petty trading and petty jobs of mechanics, welders, electricians, upholsters, painters etc. With the abolition of old vehicles and machines in the name of environment, new vehicles are replacing old ones. No repairs are needed. All these Muslims will go jobless.

The "Socialist Brahmins" had prevented this unity by catchy slogans of *Gharibi hatao, rozgar yojnas, roti kapda aur makan* and lulled them on false hopes. The honest "Sacred Brahmins" are simply not capable of all this.

So from this angle also the "Sacred Brahmins" are an ideal catalytic agent to accelerate the process of the long-stagnant Indian revolution.

Remember, it was the "Socialist Brahmin" party of Congress,

the original Brahminical party of India, that caused every problem:-partition of India, the Kashmir crisis, the Punjab blood bath of Sikhs, Babri Masjid demolition, cheating in SC/ST reservations and many more.

The Hindus of India have cunningly divided themselves into two camps: "Socialist" and "Sacred Brahmins". We have given an elaborate description of the character of both. Who is better from the point of the worst oppressed Dalits and Muslims? Or even the Backward Castes and "religious minorities" like Christians and Sikhs?

The choice must be now clear and even a child will have to agree that "Sacred Brahmins" will be better in the interest of triggering the long-delayed Indian revolution.

If this is clear it is in the interest of all Bahujans (SC/ST/BCs & Muslim/Christian/Sikhs) to help the more honest "Sacred Brahmins" to grow and give it all-out support to expand and grow. Because more it grows, its thirst for blood will grow. And there will be more wars and violence which we will have to welcome.

Beginning of Indian revolution

To repeat, the real battle will begin only when the "Sacred Brahmins" get tough with Muslims declaring India a *Hindu Rashtra*. This will force them to forge Dalit-Muslim unity. Once the nazis reach this stage, they will then come to their real enemy, the Dalits. That will be the beginning of Indian revolution.

The Dalits and Backward Castes have been for too long in slumber because of the *karma* theory which has been injected deep into their blood. The *hinduisation* of this people has been going on in a big way for centuries so that they will not rebel and revolt. They will lose their patience and revolt only when they are violently tackled. So far this Hindu violence is confined only to Muslims and Christian. Once the "Sacred Brahmins" grow and expand, their real target will be Dalits who will then turn against the "Sacred Brahmins".

So, in our interest and in the interest of sharpening the contradictions and hastening the long-delayed Indian revolution we have to support the "Sacred Brahmins".

A political experiment on these lines is going on in UP under the Bahujan Samaj Party (BSP) which accepted my analysis of the Hindu society and division of Hindus into "Socialist" and "Sacred Brahmins". And then tried to use the "Sacred Brahmins" to kill the "Socialist Brahmins".

U.P. political experiment

This experiment was tried thrice before in UP. Though the BSP Government could not continue for long, its flirting with the "Sacred Brahmins" (BJP) resulted in the growth of the BSP. It grew at the expense of the "Sacred Brahmin" party (BJP). This experiment is fully in keeping with our thesis of using one enemy to kill the more dangerous enemy.

The "Socialist Brahmins" ruled India for over 50 years. None could dislodge them. What havoc they caused we have listed above. The "Sacred Brahmins" came to power only recently. Just to deceive us, the "Sacred Brahmins" are saying that they consider the "Socialist Brahmins" as their enemy. This is false. They shout at each other and fight during the day time but when the night falls both drink together, eat together and sleep together. Both are two sides of the same coin. We know it but in the interest of sharpening the contradictions we have to take sides and support the "Sacred Brahmins" to kill the "Socialist Brahmins". Use one enemy to kill the other enemy. Use thorn to remove the thorn. This is the law of contradictions.

It is not possible to fight both the "Sacred" and "Socialist Brahmins" together. It is not possible because both are same with two different names. But when they get divided politically and put on a posture and public show, we can sharpen the division by joining the one section ("Sacred Brahmins"). This is called strategy by which alone we can bring about a clash and conflict between them.

The "Sacred Brahmins" cannot come to power without the support of Dalits and BCs. If our people become ideologically perfect in the thesis I have propounded here, we can bargain with the "Sacred Brahmins" and finish the "Socialist Brahmins", the more dangerous party.

Loyal dogs

The nazis will take up Dalits, whom they consider as their blood enemy, only after they finish with the Muslims. A worm like Narendra Modi may jump today thinking that he has become a great Hindu hero by killing 2,000 odd Muslims in Gujarat Genocide-2002. But this Backward Caste worm has forgotten that a bigger worm, Kalyan Singh, a Backward Caste Lodha, as Chief Minister of UP had scored a much greater victory by demolishing the Babri Masjid (1992) that actually inaugurated the Hindu nazi era in India.

The *vaidiks* have no value for worms. A *vaidik* respects none other than a *vaidik*. Kalyan Singh was booted out. Bangaru Laxman, a Dalit, was kicked out. Vaghela, also a BC, was necked out. No person however great he may be will be spared. All worms will be used and thrown out after squeezing them dry. Even Gandhi was shot dead like a dog after he crowned a *vaidik* as India's first Prime Minister. Vivekananda was used as a foot soldier to propagate and popularise their Hinduism. The list is too long.

Dr. Ambedkar prediction

Narendra Modi will remember all these things only when he is shoed out and his head is cut. All these unthinking SC/ST/BCs licking the *vaidik* shoes will be the first to be kicked and slaughtered. Indian history has produced any number of loyal slaves like Hanuman.

The only person who has made a thorough study of the *vaidik* wicked brain and gave us all the warnings, directions and also weapons is Dr. Babasaheb Ambedkar. He is our model. He has predicted that only the Dalits, the born revolutionaries, will ultimately fight and defeat the Hindu nazis. The only thing we are waiting for is the stage when Dalits will be whipped up from their current deep slumber, made to get angry and then fight.

We are waiting for that day when the *Hindutva* — now modified into *Moditva* — bares its fangs and starts its attack on Dalits who are the blood enemies of Aryan *vaidiks*. Only when such an attack on Dalits begin, they will wake up and fight back. That day is not far off. Once the Hindu nazis "finish" the Muslims, the next stage is the Dalits.

Concluding, I once again remind our people that Brahmins had never faced defeat ever since they destroyed Budhism. The only people who can defeat them are the Dalits. But Dalits are today in deep slumber. A sort of coma. Slaves enjoying their slavery. They have to be whipped up from this sleep. And the Modis, Togadias, Bal Thackerays will do this job. That is why we have to support the "Sacred Brahmins" in our own interest. ■

* * *

CHAPTER - XV

Stop worshipping Aryan gods

The entire history of India is undergoing a cruel surgical operation. It is being twisted out of shape and even such a well-established and a historically-proved fact like the Aryan invasion of India is being erased to say that Aryans are also indigenous. Even Dr. Babasaheb Ambedkar who, in all his voluminous writings and speeches published by the Maharashtra Government in 17 volumes, has repeatedly asserted that Aryans are foreigners and invaders, is being deliberately misquoted to say just the opposite based on one sole single sentence in his book, *Who Were the Shudras*. (DV Sept.16, 2003 p.19: "*Dr. Ambedkar never changed his opinion on Aryans*", Ranjit Kumar Biswas).

Riddles of Rama & Krishna

The Aryans, who today go by the recently popularised name of Hindus, are trying to tailor history to their current needs. Till very recently the Aryans were proudly announcing their foreign origin but the advent of parliamentary democracy, in which the numbers count, put them on the defensive. They have corrupted and co-opted many indigenous "historians" to sing their song. But all their multi-million rupee project to re-write the Indian history (and also steal and destroy the ancient reference books in libraries) will not succeed because the world has already taken note of these historical facts and nothing on earth can erase the well-embedded memories which is the other word for history.

Having said this much, I want to briefly state certain facts that India which is a vast country of villages is still free from the Aryan contamination and the village-dwelling people continue to be pure and simple Dravidians still living in peace but confined to their "nation" (caste or subcaste). No Aryan influence has penetrated into the steal-frame of caste.

The two famous terms, *Dasa* and *Dasyu*, repeatedly mentioned with great contempt in the Brahminical texts refer to those powerful indigenous tribal units who tried to destroy the Aryans and their gods. Because the Aryan gods, unlike the peace-loving gods of the indigenous people, were destructive and had hardly any divine trace in them. Dr. Ambedkar makes this clear in his book, *Riddles in Hinduism* (*W&S*, Vol.4, Maharashtra Govt., 1987) wherein he has devoted a chapter for the two most popular Hindu gods, Rama and Krishna. (*Riddle of Rama & Krishna*, DSA - 1995).

Brahmin kills Bali

The greatest *Dasyu*, hated most by the Aryans, was the famous Bali Chakravarti, whose name is remembered even to this day in every village throughout the length and breadth of India. The principal god of the Brahmins, Vishnu, killed Bali (as the legend goes) disguising himself as a dwarf Brahmin, named Vamana. All over India the killing of India's greatest Dravidian king who humbled the Aryans and made their life miserable is mourned even to this day, year after year, as *Bali Padya* (in Kerala it is called Onam). Elsewhere it is called "Diwali" or "Deepavali". Once a year Bali visits the "earth" to see his children who welcome him with lighted earthen lamps and sing his praise and dance. India's most famous "Hindu festival" called "Diwali" in North and "Deepavali" in South is in memory of Bali but corrupted by the Aryans and again twisted out of shape to erase our memories of our illustrious forefather whom the Aryan killed.

Ravana, king of Lanka, was the most famous enemy of Aryans.

Ravana conquered the whole of India from the Aryans and reduced them to abject subjection from which they were saved by the Aryan god, Rama. Ravana is hated by the Brahmins but the fact is Ravana is the saviour of Dravidians and worshipped as god in many villages of India. (Dr. B.R. Ambedkar: *Riddle of Rama & Krishna*, Vol.4, *Writings & Speeches*, 1987).

Ram Lila & burning of Ravana

It is during the Dasara festival, the Aryans burn Ravana in a public show and Delhi has its famous Ram Lila ground where our own people are employed to burn our hero Ravana and dance and rejoice over the burning.

If our historical memories say that Ravana was so great and a benevolent king, loved by the people, why our own people go to burn Ravana at the *Ram Lila* festival? It may be in the interest of the Aryans to burn Ravana because he protected Sita, who was deserted by her husband, and defended the Dravidians. As a great Budhist king Ravana fought the Aryans and their beastly culture but the Aryans don't get directly involved in the burning ceremony. All those who are engaged in the actual burning of Ravana are the very children of Ravana. A cultural revolution has to begin from here by educating our people on the real intentions behind the *Ram Lila*. Here comes Dr. Ambedkar's *Three Commandments*, "Educate, Agitate, Organise". When our people are "educated" on Ravana and Bali they will get "agitated" and this agitation in their minds will force them to "organise" against any such mischief like *Ram Lila*.

The Hindu god Rama also killed Vali (brother of Sugriva) by hiding behind a tree. The Aryans ridiculed Vali saying that he was a monkey. Brahmin texts ridiculed these powerful Dravidian kings as Rakshasa, Vanara, Daitya, Pishachi etc.

The undivided Indian subcontinent was a land flowing with milk and honey during the reign of Bali Chakravarti. It continued to be so far a long time despite the Aryan invasion which met with stiff resistance from our great tribal kings belonging to the different ethnic identities like the Mallas.

Phoolan Devi, the indigenous feminist leader

The great indigenous feminist leader, Phoolan Devi, described as a dacoit by the Aryans for killing the Thakurs who gang-raped her but later elected to Parliament by her own people but shot dead by her Aryan foes, belonged to this great Malla race. Budha, a great non-Aryan saint, was connected with the Mallas (Gustav Oppert: *The Dravidians*, Asian Educational Services, PO Box 4534, New Delhi - 110 016, 1988).

The Mahars, once the rulers of Maharashtra, were also Mallas. None of these tribal units ever accepted the Aryan rule, their supremacy, or their customs or their gods. Even to this day. The entire South India is anyway free from Aryan contamination.

Another powerful Tamil Untouchable ethnic race called Pallar is also derived from Malla. Paraiahs are yet another powerful ethnic race. In Karnataka, they are called Holeya. All these original inhabitants of India never worshipped the Aryan gods. They had their own deities which they worship even to this day. The chief village goddess is a female deity called Maramma which is worshipped in all South Indian villages. It is the Untouchables who pull the temple cart even to this day at Melkote, a Brahmin temple in Mandya dt. of Karnataka. They enter the Melkote temple for three days in every year. The different Untouchable castes like the Mang (Maharashtra), Madiga (AP and Karnataka) are corruption of the word Matang. The Untouchable Paraiahs produced the country's greatest saint-philosopher, Thiruvalluvar, who wrote the world's longest poetry called the *Thirukkural*. Thiruvalluvar lived in Madras (Mylapore).

Pulaya connection with Padmanabha temple

The Pulayas are the single largest Untouchable caste of Kerala who produced the great Ayyankali. The famous Padmanabha temple at Trivandrum was connected with Pulayas, according to Gustav Oppert. (ibid p. 76-77).

The Aryan population of India continues to be very small even to this day — a micro-minority. Gustav Oppert quoting the 1881 Census Report puts the Aryan population at 13,693,439 as against the total population of the undivided India at 252,541,210. This figure has slightly gone up with the partition of India. But the point to be noted here the Aryans (who today can be equated with Hindus) include the different *shudra* castes who form the bulk of the Hindu population. Though the *shudras* form the fourth and the last *varna* of the four-fold *varna* order, they are as much hostile to Brahmins despite being corrupted and co-opted to the Brahminical system. The famous non-Brahmin movement of the pre-independence days was led by the *shudra* races.

Experts say the different *shudra* castes like the Jats are not Aryan and hence can't be clubbed with Hindus. The *shudras* are as hostile to Brahmins as the Untouchable races. That means the Hindu population of India is about 15% including the *shudras* who form the single largest chunk.

But with the advent of "independence", which conferred the rulership on Brahmins, thanks to the efforts of M.K. Gandhi, they started distorting (if not destroying) history making us believe through their media and textbooks that Hinduism (Brahminism) is the religion of India and their gods are Hindu.

A correct reading of history will reveal the falsity of their claim.

Before the advent of Aryans what was the religion of India? This question can be answered with a counter-question. What was the religion of Europe before it became Christian? What was the religion of Africans before Christianity and Islam went there? People all over the world had their own religion and deities before organised religions were born. Indians also belonged to the same category. They belonged to no organised religion. They worshipped nature, village deities (*Gram-Devatas*). That does not mean they had no religion or no god. They all believed in god and led a spiritual life for centuries. Budhism and Jainism had all-India sweep before the Aryan religion (if it can be called a religion) spread its influence.

Gram-Devatas

Village deities (*Gram-Devatas*) with minor exceptions are all female as against Hindu gods which are only male. The indigenous people had their own priests. This is so all over India even to this day in all the villages. Brahminism is confined to urban areas only. The villages are in tact even to this day — pure and unadulterated. Ancestor worship is a special feature of the Dravidian India (Henry Whitehead, *The Village Gods of South India*, 1921 - Asian Educational Services, C-2/15, SDA, New Delhi - 110 016). Side by side with the older cults of the village deities, the Brahminical cult gradually made its inroads as centuries passed. But the village deities accompanied by the animal sacrifice were closer to the hearts of village India. This is the case in the whole of India even to this day.

Realising the great influence of village gods, the Brahmins tried to co-opt many of them. Siva was the most important god whom the Brahmins co-opted although giving him the last place in their trinity of Brahma, Vishnu, Maheswara. Because the entire country worshipped Shiva, the Brahmins had no other alternative but to accept him as part of the trinity. The Brahmins put the total number of their gods at 330 million and most of their gods are co-opted from the Dravidian village gods. Corrupting and co-opting is one of the most powerful weapons of Brahminism and many powerful village gods fell victim to this process. Brahminism started to gradually swallow the ancient religion and culture of the indigenous people. This process called *Sanskritisation* is going on even to this day though not with much success. In spite of such a reckless *Sanskritisation*, over 80% of the people of India still stick to their *Gram-Devatas*. In some places the two systems exist side by side.

Puri, Tirupati temples

Brahminism is expert in adapting and absorbing anything that is hostile to its interests. It freely borrowed from the native ceremonies, deities. Most of the Brahminical customs, rituals, music, dance, even their gods are stolen from the indigenous people. The famous Jagannath temple at Puri was a tribal shrine. Today's famous Hindu temple at Tirupati, Sabarimalai, Madurai were all Budhist shrines.

What we today call as Hindu temples are themselves stolen from the indigenous people. Temple is the result of a long process of development which spreads over several centuries, says N. Venkata Ramanayya (*An Essay on the Origin of the South Indian Temples*, 1930, Methodist Publishing House, Madras).

His research reveals that most of the temples were originally graves and tombs around which temples grew. The grave became a temple. The original religion of the Dravidians consisted of the worship of ancestral spirits and village gods.

As the Aryan contacts developed, their *Sanskritisation* process cast its net on these shrines and the Dravidian religions gradually got Aryanised:

> "The so-called Aryan temple was an institution borrowed by the Aryans from Dravidian inhabitants of Northern India". (Ibid. p.78). His conclusion is "every part of our temple had an indigenous origin" (Ibid. p. 79).

Dr. Babasaheb Ambedkar called this process as Brahminical counter-revolution which began centuries ago with their destruction of Budhism and driving it out of India.

Cultural revolution

If we have to reverse this process, it will be possible only through a powerful cultural revolution which can be triggered through the triple process of "Educate, Agitate, Organise" (Dr. Ambedkar's Three Commandments, DSA).

The Aryans having become the rulers of India since "independence", they have taken not only full charge of every section of the society but have established their powerful hold on the media, education system and public opinion which is at their command. So it is a super human task to reverse the process. The cult of Rama was unleashed on the indigenous people who were used to demolish the Babri Masjid (1992). This proves how powerful is the Aryan propaganda machinery and their mind-controlling apparatus.

Aryans don't hate Muslims

But their targets were urban centres which are in a minority. Villages are still free from Brahminical contamination. Their *hinduisation* process may be galloping but they have failed to demolish and destroy the caste. In fact the institution of caste is strengthening. The Hindu nazi party of BJP itself is divided on caste basis. The Brahminical forces have succeed only on one front: that is killing the Muslims by using their religion. But the Muslims are not the enemy of Aryans. During the 1,000-year Muslim rule Brahmins loyally served the Muslims. The Aryans are rousing emotions and instigating the indigenous people against Muslims not because they hate the Muslims. They think that by making the Dalits to kill and burn the Muslims and their places of worship, the indigenous people will become "good Hindus". Their aim is to enslave the indigenous people totally in which they have not succeeded. The indigenous people become "good Hindu" only while attacking Muslims but the moment the anti-Muslim war and violence are over they revert back to their caste cocoon (ethnic identity). This is what is worrying the Aryans. Caste is killing casteism (Hinduism). They want to kill the caste (our ethnic identity) and at the same time maintain casteism which is the other word for Hinduism. But that is not happening. In fact, caste consolidation and *caste identity* are getting strengthened. This is a great development to which *Dalit Voice* can rightly claim some credit.

Periyar was not against indigenous gods

While it may be difficult for the weak indigenous people to counter the powerful Aryan ruling forces, it is still possible for them to bend if not break the Aryan upsurge by stopping the worship of Aryan gods. At least the conscious sections among us can set the example by launching a campaign in our areas of influence.

That does not mean we must stop believing in god. Not at all. That is not my argument. What I say is we should stop worshipping Aryan gods. The Aryan gods are not our gods. Not only that. They are against us and our very existence. They caused our enslavement. This is the opinion of all philosophers and historians. Why should we leave and forget our own gods who love us and take to our enemy gods? Even Periyar E.V. Ramaswamy — hailed as the most famous atheist of the 20th century India — nowhere spoke against our indigenous gods. He attacked only the Aryan gods. When he asked the people to "throw out the gods", he meant only the Aryan gods. (Periyar E.V. Ramaswamy, *The Salvation to Shudra Slavery*, DSA-1986).

All the indigenous people have their own village deities. These village deities continue to be our reigning gods even now. In my village of South Kanara (in coastal Karnataka), we have our *Bhootas* (ancestor worship). They are powerful deities even today. In my ancestral house (Vontibettu Beedu), there was no Aryan god till I completed my graduation (1955). What we had in our house was *Bhootada Mancha* (a wooden platform for the *Bhoota* - our ancestral Bhoota is Kalkuda) and a *Bhootada Kone* (a room for the Bhoota). I have never seen any portrait or idol of any Brahmin god. This is so all over my district. My study, travel, experience (coupled with what my elders told me) reveal that this is the case all over South India. Were not the people of the whole of South existing without the Aryan gods for centuries? In fact, our people had a peaceful, harmonious life. My district of South Kanara had never witnessed any anti-Muslim riots or any caste clash. Every caste and community lived in great harmony. There were plenty of Brahmins in the Ambalpadi village (part of Udupi town) where I went to school. The Brahmins never gave us any trouble. They never interfered with us. However, they led their secluded life and we did not mind it. We had Muslims, Christians, Backward Castes and Scheduled Castes. There was no ill-will, jealousy. Though the powerful Madhwa Brahmin centre of Udupi temple existed, the indigenous people continued with their strong belief in respective native village gods even while visiting the Udupi temple.

Why not stop worshipping the Aryan gods, which destroyed our ethnic identity and our entire cultural heritage, and go back to our indigenous village deities? It is by switching our loyalties from village deities to Aryan gods the peace, tranquility and brotherhood that existed in our society are lost.

So, in the interest of restoring peace and strengthening the unity and integrity of the country and also to purify our society by purging the Brahminical poison, we must shift back to our village gods by stopping worship of Aryan gods.

This can begin first with each individual, then spread to our household. And once the household reverts to village gods, it will catch up and a cultural movement will automatically generate. Indigenous people have to give serious thought to the revival of our great glorious, peaceful, spiritual heritage which once thrived among us but got destroyed by the commercialised, vulgarised Hindu gods who destroyed our peace and our rich values. ■

✳ ✳ ✳

CHAPTER - XVI

Conclusion

Brahminical people survive mainly by confusing us. They have their monopoly mass media to confuse and they have hired some bum-lickers from among the victims of Brahminism. So those fighting Brahminism must suffer from no confusion. In the early period of "independence", Brahminical people manufactured marxism, communism, socialism and those who fell victim were mainly the Dalits. In parts of Kerala, Bengal, Andhra Pradesh marxism still exercises lot of pull on our people. The marxist injection works only on our people. But despite being India's top marxist leaders, the injection never worked on S.A. Dange or E.M.S. Namboodiripad. Because both were Brahmins. Marxism helped strengthen Brahminism. (V.T. Rajshekar: *How Marxh Failed in Hindu India?*, DSA-1988). So all those interested in fighting Brahminism must make a study of marxist dialectics but never fall a prey to it. India's road to socialism is not through class struggle but "caste struggle" because in India class is caste.

The Brahminical people also confuse us through ecology, environment. Hundreds of NGOs have come up to fool our people and the best known outfit is Medha Patkar's "Narmada Bahcao Andolan". Beware of environmentalists, ecology heroes and heroines. (DV July 1, 1993 guest editorial: *"Enemies of Dalits taking to new business of ecology"*).

Those interested in fighting Brahminism should always use the right word, right terminology, right phrases and avoid confusing terms like "communal fascism", cultural nationalism, *Hindutva*, Hindu right, Sangh Parivar, right reactionaries. All this mean only one thing: Brahminism. These words are used by Brahminical people to confuse us. In the guise of communal fascism, *Hindutva* etc. those hiding inside are the same people. Their job is to confuse us. Our job is not to get confused but hit the nail right on the head of Brahminism and finish it in one stroke.

Brahminism survives not because of the strength of its value system or any weighty philosophical base. It is not a philosophy. It is a political weapon to keep us enslaved — surviving only because of the strategy and tactics of its *vaidik* vampire. We who are the victims of Brahminism have the right philosophy and a liberating value system but what we lack are strategies and tactics (DV Edit May 16, 1995: "*Dalit movement lacks strategies & tactics*").

In this, I have detailed only the most important strategies and tactics. If we master these strategies and tactics and cultivate a missionary zeal, we will find no difficulty to uproot Brahminism within a decade. ■